To my wife Alice,

Who reads all my stories

with long-suffering patience.

FUN Lies

The Ambassador's Leaky Bucket of Stories That Are Completely Half-True

Cover design and all images by Mark Suroviec, M.Ed.

Paperback ISBN: 9798880170555

Hardcover ISBN: 9798880423163

Kindle ASIN: B0CW1CM6M6

FUN *Lies*

The Ambassador's Leaky Bucket of Stories That Are Completely Half-True

Mark Suroviec, M.Ed.

Foreword by Jim Karwisch

CHAPTER -2

Acknowledgements

* * *

This is the part of the book where the author remembers the names of the mountains of publishing lackeys, and with forced humility, name-drops every famous person they've ever met.

FUN Lies is independently published, which means the mountains of publishing lackeys I would like to thank...is me. Mark, you are kinda awesome.

Also, no one reads this part.

I could literally thank Oprah for the hundreds of evenings we sat in her study by the fireplace discussing the editorial choices in this book. Or thank former Supreme Court Justice Ruth Bader Ginsberg for believing that my tome is the "Foundation of Democracy" and should be used as a textbook in high school civics classes.

Would anyone notice or care? Unlikely. Attached is my grandmother's family recipe for beef stroganoff. I also would like to use this opportunity to declare myself eligible for the NCAA transfer portal, NFL draft, and self-nominate for a Nobel Prize.

All jokes aside, some people have positively influenced my writing journey and should be mentioned here.

To my writer friends from the Medium humor and satire community: Philip Ogley, Debdutta Pal, Kristen Stark, Srini Balasubramaniyan, Kristine Laco, Dr. Michael Burg, Raine Lore, Patrick Eades, Matthew Clapham, Ann James, Gerald Sturgis, Robin Wilding, Victor Cardenas, Adam Robinson, Carlo Zeno, Rachel A Fefer, and the liar of all liars Smillew Rachuef. Without you and more names unmentioned, most of this book wouldn't exist.

And my delightful Tuesday Night Improv Dojo: Alexandra Goodrich, Alex Lee, John Goodrich, Monika Odzarkska, and Sylvia Li. Thanks for letting me steal the joke about farts and waffles.

Thank you to everyone else who pity-laughed at my bits or politely pretended my words were worth reading.

Final thanks to Jim Karwisch for the permission to write a *fun* book before the *serious* & *professional* one on organizational leadership and work culture. I'll always cherish all the hours you spent investing in me before being tased by Oprah's security. Cheers.

CHAPTER -1

Foreword

* * *

I am a personal friend of Mark's as well as his improv teacher and his business coach. Mark is skilled enough at typing to make enough words to fill a book-length document, and you now have a copy– a significant accomplishment in my eyes.

Eleven months ago, when Mark told me he needed this foreword written ASAP, I told him I would get right on it. Now, eleven months later, I have gotten on it. This is it. This is the foreword. You have arrived.

Mark is exactly the kind of student that every improv teacher wishes for. He is always present and brings cash. He also convinces friends to take classes, and they bring cash too, making him the best improv student I have ever had.

Mark and I live in the same town, which you will read about later in this textual documentary. If you are curious, Mark does not make fun of me. I'm one of the cool kids. If you laugh *with* him, you are friends forever. Laughing *at* someone else might make you a [*redacted.*]

Man, I really can't believe he has done it. Mark has transcended the stage and achieved what every comedian truly wishes for—a self-published book filled with half-truths and partial lies.

What else? Hmm. I've half-heartedly dedicated twelve minutes to this foreword so far, and I feel like it is solid. Should I read other forewords from other authors' books to see how it goes? But that is much more effort than this book deserves. When will I have time for Oprah's new cookbook or Michelle Obama's teen paranormal romance? I might need more than a half-hour at the keyboard for a change.

Wait.

Do you realize that for every page I write here, Mark's book extends by a page? And is it more expensive to print? Any extra writing actively removes money from Mark's pocket. I know Mark well enough to guarantee he won't charge more than the eight pennies this book is worth.

Delightful. You can call me Robin Hood. I just saved you twenty bucks on printing costs, buddy. If there aren't any words after this sentence, Mark figured out my plan and...

Well done, Mark.

Jim Karwisch

JimProv [1]

---

[1] Jim Karwisch is a Speaker, Facilitator, & Coach at *Untangled Narrative.* untanglednarrative.com

INTRODUCTION

This Book Is Half-True

* * *

I love to lie.

Not about anything important like my professional resume, where my wife thinks I slept last night, or reporting revenue to the IRS. But silly, stupid white lies about details of zero consequence? Let the games begin!

To say it another way, I love spontaneously generated playful fiction. One of my former co-workers coined the pejorative *Mark Facts* because she said, "Half of the words out of your mouth are made-up nonsense." To which I responded,

> *"Did you know that there is a college in western Pennsylvania named Slippery Rock University? The school was named during the Revolutionary War when General Norman Rock slipped away from an overwhelming force of British Redcoats. They built the university campus on top of the field where he avoided the battle."* [2]

---

[2] Real college, but a fake origin story. Want to hear something 100% true? My college competed against SRU in Track & Field. A live carp lived in the water pit of their steeplechase.

"I didn't know that," she replied.

Trying to withhold a smirk on my terrible poker face quickly gave the game away.

"Wait, is that an ACTUAL fact or a MARK Fact?"

LYING IS FUN

When I founded WorkPlay Solutions in 2021, friends, colleagues, and unfortunate bystanders in the Kroger checkout line would ask me, "What does your business do?"

Instead of telling future clients, "We make work fun and leaders more effective," something absurd would leap from my lips in its place.

"We do identity theft. Protection? No, we CAUSE identity theft. I have some great Nigerian Prince emails you can use. How many of your grandparents are still alive?"

GREAT GOOGILY MOOGILY

It wasn't until I took some improv classes from Jim Karwisch that I understood this compulsion to say the first ridiculous thing that pops into my head when people ask you a serious question. He taught me about comedy bits, timing, and the art of improvisational theater. Then it clicked.

All my life, I have been performing these short one-person shows on an imaginary stage – except – no one else knew it was a performance until it was over.

I relished the feeling of creation, telling the imaginary to the unsuspecting audience and having my story believed.

IS MARK A NARCASSIST?

To the cynical, these habits of unconsented fiction sound like an exercise of an uncaring narcissist practicing the soft skills of quick manipulation. Yes, I sought to trick, fool, and prank. Still, the desired outcome was never personal gain or feelings of superiority.

Instead, my motivation is sharing laughter and personal connection with whoever I meet. Let us create unusual memories together.

After a bit, people laughed. At me? With me? Who knows, I didn't care. These tiny moments brought me joy, seeing the unexpected smile on someone's face. Or the surprise of failed execution when the humor fell flat. Suddenly, the reward was replaced by expressions with a condescending blank stare that screams, "I think Mark is a dumb*ss."

INSIGHT

Expectations have power. If someone expects a straight answer with a straight face, then receiving tomfoolery with a straight face can bypass our filters and let the child inside come out and play. The same is true for books.

What is a plot twist but misdirection and subtle lies waiting for the climax to be revealed? If readers believe you are telling the truth, then gifted writers can lie to you, and you will thank them for it. I don't claim to be one of those talented few.

This book was written by a below-average storyteller farting words out of his mouth, stumbling towards a pot of gold at the end of the rainbow.

WHAT'S THE DEAL?

You are reading a collection of satire, shenanigans, and tomfoolery. Some stories are 100% historically accurate occurrences from my life. Others are ludicrous "what-ifs," the absurdity with no anchor in the material world. Most pieces in this anthology blend the two. You will find ridiculous lists of nonsense, pretend news in the style of the Onion or the Babylon Bee, and embellished personal narratives on the razor edge of satire.

Some of you, like my wife, will never laugh at the stupidity contained inside this book. But when you ask, "Did that *really* happen?" or "Seriously? How much of this story is true?" I've accomplished my job as an author. Look for Easter eggs, and don't take anything at face value, including the footnotes, for they may also be playful fiction. Enjoy!

Fun lies within,

Mark Suroviec, M.Ed.

Ambassador of Fun

CHAPTER 1

Trust Me, I'm Not a Doctor

* * *

Dear Not-a-Doctor Mark is a monthly humor column where the non-guru incorrectly answers your self-help questions on topics he doesn't fully understand.

DEAR NOT-A-DOCTOR MARK

I may have imposter syndrome. Can you help me? These feelings started when I met Garrett. We became best friends playing second string on the lacrosse team before pledging Delta Omicron Upsilon CHi Epsilon. [3]

During Spring Break '98 in Cabo, we both got wickedly drunk, stumbled into a sketchy beachside tattoo parlor, and out popped matching tats of our fraternity crest wrapped in barbed wire and the inscription #LaxBoyz.

Who was Garrett's best man when he married my high school sweetheart Gretchen? Me. Who lied on their resume to get us hired by Arborvitae Investment House LLC, a global hedge fund company? I did.

After sifting through Garrett's trash, I found his hide-a-key in a hollowed-out garden gnome and duplicated it at Ace Hardware. I use the key to housesit when his family goes on vacation — without

[3] D.O.U.C.H.E.

being asked.

His flannel jammies are sooooooooo comfy.

I added Garrett to my Spotify family plan without telling him. His computer now contains spyware to have the same Google search history and cookie settings. We have the same social security number, mother's maiden name, and bank account passwords.

Sometimes, I try to pick up our — I mean his — kids from school. Last weekend, Garrett went to a tax accounting conference, and I slept in his bed for two hours. Gretchen didn't notice. She snores like a Sharknado making babies with a Velociraptor.

$60,000 of my retirement savings was diverted to have my nose and chin surgically chiseled to look more like Garrett. I could go on and on with the list Garrett's wife made for me, which is not exhaustive.

Reading several blogs about Imposter Syndrome by online content creators with limited life experience, I'm worried I might be suffering from this cryptic and debilitating condition. What should I do?

Concerned,

— ~~Garrett~~ An Imposter

* * *

DEAR AN IMPOSTER

Great news! You are not suffering from Imposter Syndrome, but your actions are extremely sus.

Mental health professionals fail to recognize Imposter Syndrome as a legitimate condition in the DSM-5. However, experts agree your ailment may originate from gluten intolerance or a lack of healing crystals.

What you are describing is not the nebulous boogeyperson of Imposter Syndrome. Your symptoms more closely align with a retelling of the 1992 classic thriller Single White Female. The movie stars a young Jennifer Jason Leigh, who impersonates her roommate, played by Bridget Fonda. Leigh slowly overtakes Fonda's life, locking her in the apartment and stealing her boyfriend. The movie culminates in a violent altercation between the title characters, leaving Leigh dead from multiple stab wounds.

My advice? Any self-help columnist worth a glazed donut will tell you the same thing. Leigh's story did not end well. Bleeding out from multiple stab wounds makes it challenging to reach your full potential.

Instead, focus your energy on scriptwriting. Single White Female 2: #LaxBoyz is a movie that is dying to be made. Do any of your venture capital buddies want to bankroll the film? On that note, do you have any stock tips?

Tyler Perry should play both you and Garrett in the movie. Now, that's a twist! Would Jennifer Jason Leigh or Bridget Fonda do a cameo? I need to find an agent.

You're welcome,

— Not-a-Doctor Mark

CHAPTER 2

Let's Suck at Twitter Together

* * *

After a year on Twitter, I have eight followers.[4]

Is this some sort of record? According to Twitter guru Luca Hammer, the verified account with the least followers is @ghisperrier— with two. The profile with the most followers is @Katyperry, with a paltry 92.2 million. [5]

My Twitter existence has far more in common with @ghisperrier than Katy Perry and one hundred and thirty-four FEWER followers than the parody vaping company @DepressionStick.

Did Luca's attention bring sudden stardom to old Ghispy? Nope, the enigmatic battery king shut down that BirdX account.

---

[4] Mark wrote this story before Twitter became "X." He dreams one hundred years in the future and our robot overlords still call it Twitter–at least in this galaxy.

[5] Twitter research from 2016. In 2022, Luca and Katy married and now live in Jeff Bezo's underground castle.

THE TORCH OF TERRIBLE

Does the torch of the terrible pass to me? Is my online presence the Twitter equivalent of a dank and moldy underground lair? We are not describing the awe-inspiring multi-billion dollar, high-tech complex where supervillains live. It's a radioactive, sewage-tainted cave that spells like Aunt Stella cooked Brussels sprouts for six hours.

Is Luca sitting in his infinity pool, dishing up cyber burns to my account now that I'm in last place? He could be, and I would never know.

Am I to flame out before my tweeting prime and never make an impact? Will parents warn their children of me? Will those same children dress like me for Halloween? A more horrifying spectacle than Sexy Bill Belichick? [6]

None of my other social media is this inept. I did not have Instagram before starting my business. I put in the time and learned anyway. But for whatever reason, my will to tweet is lacking.

#INEPT_IN_THE_TWITTERVERSE

If I suck at Twitter and you suck at Twitter, can we help each other? And by help, I mean we cheat. What if we follow each other—not to benefit society? Is this idea groundbreaking, worn out, or a violation of the unwritten rules of social media? No idea.

---

[6] Bill Belichick is a future hall-of-fame football coach with a long tenure at the New England Patriots. My editor removed the disturbing AI-generated image of *Sexy Bill Belichick*. "Can never unsee that horror," she mumbled.

WHY CHEAT?

Shouldn't we learn from someone who knows what they are doing? Absolutely not. If we get real help, we must put in authentic effort. Who wants to be Katy Perry? I do not, nor do you—for several reasons, and none of them have to do with Twitter.

My manhood is not measured by likes or social media following. However, I am tired of being embarrassed by the number eight.

My head shakes at influencers reposting dad jokes with half the world's attention. Are you fed up and fake angry as much as I am? Probably not. If you were, you would tweet about it, and people would listen.

Can we bag a few Twitter followers together with little effort? So go ahead and add @workplaysol. I have no standards–you know I'll follow you. [7]

---

[7] Be kind. I put as much effort into this story as I do on Twitter.

CHAPTER 3

Yelp Review of the Water Park First Aid Station

* * *

"Bandages covered a full 70% of my open head wound. Superb!"

THE WATER SLIDE

He loves how fearless his four-year-old daughter is on intense carnival rides. She resembles a Valkyrie, destined for the glories of Valhalla, towering over the amusement park's height requirements by a mere half-inch.

"See! I'm tall enough. I can be brave, Daddy." She assures him.

The father looks up at the multi-floor staircase to reach the pinnacle of the water slide, partially hidden by the clouds.

"Are you sure, honey? The Vitamix Turbo Thunder Whirlpool Human Blender of Death and Destruction sounds like a scary ride. It's tall and goes much faster than the slides we did earlier."

"Daddy, I can be brave."

"Let's do it!" He's the fun dad. "You go first."

THE ASCENT

The fun dad and his zealous offspring hike up the stairs, only stopping to change oxygen tanks above 14,000 ft. At the summit peak, the Lifeguard-Sherpa greets the pair with the enthusiasm of a bored teenager listening to music on his AirPods — because he is a bored teenager listening to music on his AirPods.

The intrepid travelers patiently wait for their turn to descend the several hundred-mile slaloms down the hydrated fiberglass channel in donut-shaped inner tubes.

Another father admires the look of determination in the young girl's eyes. “I'm impressed. I couldn't get my son to go. And he's seven.”

The fun dad lifts his chin and puffs out his chest, reeking of pride. “She's only four!” taking a moment to be smug. “I win at parenting,” he mumbles to himself.

THE DECSENT

“It's my turn, Daddy.”

With her internal stores of bravery at the max capacity, she rockets down the slide at twice the speed of sound. A sonic boom bellows, disrupting the other thrill seekers of the forgotten lakefront RV campground. The Ambassador sees his daughter reach the splash landing filled with joy and without incident.

“Is it my turn?” He says to the Sherpa, whose dead eyes show no recognition of human speech.

GO?

The fun dad feels the wind in his hair plummeting his tube down the water slide approaching the speed of light. Enveloped by the speed bubble and with flames trailing him like a rogue comet, gravity powers his manic acceleration.

In a trance, he reflects on the mysteries of life and the universe. "Let's play a game." His altered consciousness declares.

It's called,

Let's Ride the Extreme Water Slide–Flip Upside Down and Hit My Head–Bleed Everywhere, and Test the First Aid Skills of the Lifeguards.

"Sounds like a good idea to me," his body responds before the message clears his prefrontal cortex.

WHACK!

"F**k," his mouth erupts as he slides head first down the shute without his fickle inner tube. His daughter looks on in horror, hearing that word from her father's lips for the first time. [8]

The fun dad's wife rushes onto the scene as he crawls out of the slide and lies on the ground.

"Are you ok? Oh s**t, you're bleeding."

He tries to signal the mountaintop lifeguard, but his urgent communication is ignored. His wife rushes off to find medical attention, and before long, water park staff escort him to a waiting

---

[8] You should never swear around young and impressionable children — but get a free pass during unexpected head injuries.

area for treatment.

How was my visit to the first aid station at Captain Pirate's Aqua Park and Redneck Slide-o-rama? Let's look at the pros and cons listed below:

PROS

- Safety — Lifeguards wore nitrile gloves to prevent exposure to blood-borne pathogens, which was pretty smart because I lost a lot of blood.
- The I ❤ Hot Dads t-shirt worn by female staff conveys a sense of professionalism and medical expertise.
- Lifeguards demonstrated quality patient care by using humor to diffuse a stressful situation.
- Bandages covered a full 70% of my open head wound. Superb!
- The manager was confident he bought appropriately sized bandages this summer, and they were somewhere on the property — just not inside the first aid kit.
- The highly trained staff were able to quickly rule out the possibility of a concussion by not knowing how to test for a concussion.

CONS

- ❖ Lousy response time.
- ❖ The slide operator ignored my wild, erratic gestures, alerting him of the emergency. However, my hand signals could easily be interpreted. *After I finish with this swarm of bees, I want to fight you in the parking lot.*
- ❖ Awkward Florence Nightingale moment in front of my wife where a lifeguard suggestively revealed her hot dad shirt was "kinda true."
- ❖ They were out of ice, so I borrowed a misshapen freezer pack from a friend's beer cooler.

OVERALL EXPERIENCE | 3.5 STARS

"Superb for a redneck RV campground amusement park."

Word of advice? Never sign the liability waiver.[9]

---

[9] The preceding story was an authentic account of my water park experience, with some details exaggerated for comic effect. The head injury, inappropriate t-shirt, and patient care all happened. If you are wondering, I'm fully recovered from the incident.

CHAPTER 4

27 Free Burns For the Creatively Impaired

* * *

Do you have a hard time mocking others or delivering witty comebacks? Is your default comeback "You Suck"? Instead of spouting off uninspired slams, try these novel put-downs instead.

SIDEBURNS

- Not saying she's old, but when your momma was born, people still rode camels to work and milked yaks before sunrise.
- Your face looks like the producers of Sesame Street made Cookie Monster eat gluten-free biscuits made of asparagus and thumbtacks.
- 4 out of 5 Karens think you are bats**t crazy.
- While it is no longer considered appropriate to body shame another person, I feel compelled to violate this social norm in your case. COMPELLED!
- You remind me of someone who spray tans frequently.
- Every time you speak, millions of climate activists question the wisdom of saving the planet. Thanks to you, Greta Thunberg is flying a private plane to Antarctica to melt icebergs with a blowtorch.
- Who urinated in your Lucky Charms?
- No ONE is saying you're stupid. She's at least a SIX.
- Are you the same person who complained that she couldn't listen to my podcast in Braille?
- I would rather spend a fourteen-hour flight to Paris with a miniature baby screeching inside my ear canals than hear the next word out of your mouth.

SUNBURNS

- ❖ Turn that frown upside-up.
- ❖ Your job sounds sooooo hard — like you have to walk eleven miles uphill both ways in the snow before taking Zoom calls in Cookie Monster pajamas.
- ❖ Tired? Looks like someone didn't have their dairy-free almond buttermilk extract kale-infused Keto-blast meta booster smoothie this morning.
- ❖ When people see your Tinder profile, they don't swipe left — they smash their phone with a boot, like in spy movies.
- ❖ You remind me of a chihuahua that dry-humped the Statue of Liberty.
- ❖ When I was your age, we sat in an office with real CHAIRS — not a treadmill desk or human hamster ball.
- ❖ You forgot the last two words of the phrase. It's not "Nobody wants to work anymore." It's "Nobody wants to work anymore — with you."
- ❖ Frown that turn downside-out.
- ❖ 4 out of 5 Cookie Monsters would urinate in Braille on your Zoom call.
- ❖ I would rather spray tan a miniature baby than eat a gluten-free Greta Thunberg.

CHEMICAL BURNS

- ❖ Your argument makes a particular former U.S. President sound stable and coherent.
- ❖ Out of all the sperm racing to the zygote finish line, how was YOURS the winner?
- ❖ When I was Karen's age, 5 out of 4 people urinated in their spray tans.
- ❖ Remember that horror movie where the protagonist was trapped in a sewer and had to cut off her arm to escape because the saw blade was too dull to cut the shackles? I am that woman — you are that saw.
- ❖ I would rather move to Paris inside a human hamster ball than spray-tan the Statue of Liberty.
- ❖ 4 out of 5 Greta Thunbergs frown topside-out at miniature baby camels.
- ❖ Sorry, Karen. My milk-yak spilled thumbtacks in your pajamas. But you deserved it. [10]

---

[10] This list of ludicriosity was my attempt to emulate the brilliant style of humor writer Srini Balasubramaniyan. Unfortunately, my awkward attempts will leave the reader embarrassingly unsatisfied— like with every woman I ever dated.

CHAPTER 5

How to Fail at Making Coffee

* * *

WARNING: The following story makes Mark Suroviec appear less intelligent than he is. Or reveals he is much dumber than he believes.

I attempted to brew coffee this morning with a single-serve coffee machine and failed.

I am mortified. My coffee maker is so uncomplicated that a naked mole rat could brew a perfect Sumatra without watching any MoleTube video tutorials. How can any human screw up a coffee machine with only one button?

WHAT HAPPENED

I should have placed a coffee mug underneath the dispenser before putting in the coffee pod and pressing the start button.

I did not.

Instead, twelve liquid ounces of mahogany-colored caffeine gold poured over the kitchen counter, cabinets, and floor.

Our floor was stickier than after cake time at a toddler's birthday party. The newspaper was thoroughly coffee-logged. Even worse, my exceedingly rare bobblehead collection of Former

British Prime Ministers Dressed as Professional Wrestlers lost their mint-in-a-box status.

In a daze, I carried the café machinery to the sink. Failing to understand cause & effect, gravity, and other laws of physics, I tipped the coffee maker upside down to drain the spillage. The entire water reservoir drenched my clothing.

I stood there sadly by myself — in the world's least appealing wet t-shirt contest — wondering how the situation escalated so quickly.

CATCH-22

How on earth do I clean up all this mess? With an ironic laugh, I realized I could think my way out of this situation if only I had some coffee. But to make coffee, I had to tidy up the mess and reboot the wet machine without getting electrocuted.

HOW I GOT ELECTROCUTED

I scrubbed the kitchen and coffee machine using paper towels and bleach wipes. The tongs on the power cord were incredibly sticky. I wiped them off and plugged the device into the electrical outlet when...

ZAP!!!

...the coffee machine turned on as intended, with no unexpected power surges. Were you expecting me to get electrocuted? What's wrong with you? All I wanted this morning was a steaming cup of Joe, and your sadistic mind hoped for me to receive flesh-sizzling personal injuries.

Don't try to defend yourself. Don't try to tell me unrelated nonsense like, "Mark, you literally wrote HOW I GOT ELECTROCUTED."

You can't blame me for the darkness of your soul. The condition of your heart is evil gelatinous goo, and it scares me.[11]

[11] Authors Note: Delete the last few paragraphs of rambling paranoia after I drink more coffee.

CHAPTER 6

Betrayed By Scrabble

* * *

Does the path lead to destruction or redemption?

THE ANDERSCHMITTS

Archibald Anderschmitt sat alone in his tweed smoking jacket, wondering how to tell his children the truth. "Pants. First, I need to put on pants," he mumbled, lacking enthusiasm. He staggered into the living room, where three generations of his family gathered for their Boxing Day traditions.

Archibald, the eldest living member of the Anderschmitt clan, surveyed the room. Five children and fourteen grandchildren scurried around the vast living room of his Tudor estate. He eyed Charity, his eldest daughter, as she chased 10-month-old twins crawling across the perfectly waxed floor.

"Keep those Legos away from the twins!" She shouted at her husband. Charles mumbled an unrecognizable response from the sofa, half-asleep, watching a mediocre hockey game on the flat screen above the fireplace.

Arch scanned the room and saw everyone he expected except the man next to 16-year-old Bella, his rebellious granddaughter. "The man, no boy, next to her must be her new boyfriend," he mused. "I guess I have to include him too," stifling his gallows humor laugh.

"Dad?" awoke Arch from his brief revelry. "Dad? Don't just stand there. Join us. It's almost time to open presents," said his impatient daughter Kimberly.

THE CONFESSION

Hesitating, he found his tongue stuck to the roof of his mouth like the time he accidentally ate peanuts at Kimberly's wedding and Grace stabbed him with an EpiPen.

"Oh, Grace. I would never have gotten into this pit if you were still alive." His thoughts betrayed the hopelessness he felt confronting his family.

The older children looked up from their phones, sensing a change in the room's atmosphere. What was joyful and full of holiday spirit seemed to leech away into the winter winds outside.

"I have a confession to make," he said.

The last words came out as a suppressed cough. The room quieted, and Charity poked the slouching Charles in the ribs. The retort on Charles's lips died as he saw his wife mouth the words, "It's important."

The attention was back on the family patriarch, who feared to speak and cursed himself for his lack of courage.

"It's gone. It's all gone," his voice barely whispered in the chilly room.

"Grandpa, what's gone?" Bella spoke to the waiting family.

"Everything. My bank accounts, subsidiary companies, and retirement funds – erased. Our land, this house, and even your college fund are gone. We are broke."

Shocked reactions cascaded throughout the room and

manifested into chaos. Charity gasped. Kimberly slapped the coffee table, inadvertently tossing more Legos at the younger children. The twins' crying started slowly, gaining momentum like a WW2-era air raid siren.

Charles jumped out of his seat on the sofa. "You lying old penis-infested douche-mop! I need that money! In all my years of putting up with a sanctimonious father-in-law, I never guessed you would screw over your entire family."

Shocked at her husband's venomous outburst, Charity slapped him.

"What Charles meant to say is, 'What happened? Where did all the money go?'"

The seconds slagged by, adding pulsating tension to every adult in the room. Arch finally spoke.

THE STORY

"Scrabble. It was High-Stakes Scrabble." He said with his hand raised, forestalling questions.

Ever since Grace died, I've felt so alone. The spark of life was missing its secret sauce. Then, one day, I had a visitor at my lowest of lows. My trusted confidant and lifelong sage of wisdom, Hobart Tennison, invited me on a spiritual journey.

He took me to this Buddhist Temple deep in the interior of Laos. We walked by the pious monks, and one of them winked at me.

Hob pulled a business card out of his pocket with only one word.

OXYPHENBUTAZONE?

The monk smiled when he saw the card and pulled some creeping vines apart, revealing a trap door. Hobart and I descended wooden stairs caked in the dusk, and he answered my unspoken query.

"It's a 15-letter word that results in 1778 points if you play it in Scrabble. Where we are going, it matters."

"If you say so," I mumbled, unconvinced.

The descending stairs ended in a cave of rough-hewn granite. I'm still unsure if we walked through that cave for hours or minutes. Reaching the cave's tapering end wall, I heard machinery.

THE DEN OF DEBAUCHERY

My eyes adjusted to the light and saw a glorious casino hidden from the rest of the world.

"What in the unholy sweet mother of pickles is this place?" I said louder than intended.

"Welcome to our den of debauchery," a horned figure in a red tuxedo intoned in his singsong voice.

"We have a game of chance for every vice,

and will not rest until we entice."

My eyes adjusted to the bright lights that were such a difference from the dimness of the cave. I peered around the room and saw the traditional games–Blackjack, Roulette, Texas Hold-Em Poker. Then it got weird.

WHISPERS IN THE LIGHT

Is that Monopoly? Risk? Mousetrap?

I squinted and saw two elderly Asian men in fine suits placing bets on orangutans handling Jenga blocks.

Four young women in cocktail dresses gathered around a Plinko board twice the size of the original from The Price is Right. I looked closer and saw the pegs were made of human thumbs, not wood.

There was an entire room predicting how many farts per minute an acne-covered high school boy would deal after eating a gas station burrito. My hands touched my face reflexively, remembering my childhood pox scars.

As my muse called me from across the gambling paradise, the acne room lost color and sound. It sought out my mind. It knew my name. It owned my soul.

SCRABBLE

As I walked towards the glamourous golden tiles, Hob stifled his obnoxious "I told you so" smirk.

"You know me better than I know myself, Hobart. I should have never doubted you." Around the table were Matthew McConaughey, Emma Watson, Dua Lipa, and Elvis.

"Elvis? Give me the flu and launch a dozen snot rockets! You're Elvis F***ing Presley."

"If I had a nickel for every time I hear those exact words," chuckled Elvis.

I stared at the empty chair as yesterday's stars picked their tiles.

"It's just a friendly gentlemen's game," Elvis said without preamble. Emma rolled her eyes at his dated remark.

HIGH STAKES AND LATE NIGHTS

We played into the night and the next day. I don't remember when my losing streak started. But I couldn't stop. The farther I fell behind, the more alive I became. It was like Redbull, coyote urine, and Tabasco sauce all flooded my veins, fighting for pulmonary supremacy.

Fearing collapse but confident of winning, there was one word left to play. I raided my bank accounts and called my lawyer, stockbroker, realtor, and everyone with some semblance of control over my finances.

Surprisingly, there was perfect cell reception for a demonic underground cave casino in a Laotian jungle. Money in hand, I played my last tiles with a triple letter AND double-word score.

VOCIFEROUSLY

"203 Points. Chew on that, you over-indulged billionaires." [12]

I reached for the winnings, and Dua Lipa jabbed her stiletto heel between my fingers, drawing a trickle of blood. She gestured to the sly smile Elvis made no effort to contain. I saw him place an O, an X, and a Y. When he put the P, all the tabasco-urine energy fueling my trance congealed into the week-old fondue.

---

[12] Somewhere, an uber-nerd is reading this story and cannot move on without fact checking my point totals. Is it you?

OXYPHENBUTAZONE!

Every ounce of wealth and financial security our family had hoarded for 150 years was gone in a moment. Scrabble, my demon muse, you betrayed me!

What did I learn from that knife twist of fate? Never trust a Tennison in an underground cave casino of sin. And never bet the farm in High Stakes Scrabble against the ghost of Elvis. [13]

---

[13] How to Get Oxyphenbutazone - WSJ Scrabble aficionado Sam Chenoweth explains how he and a fellow master's student achieved the highest-scoring word. Oct 13, 2007. Wall Street Journal.

CHAPTER 7

Not-a-Doctor Mark's Definitive Guide to Romance

* * *

Dear Not-a-Doctor Mark is a monthly humor column where the non-guru incorrectly answers your self-help questions on topics he doesn't fully understand. You would know that already if you were paying attention the first time.

DEAR NOT-A-DOCTOR MARK

Can you recommend a swanky restaurant for Valentine's Day? My fiancé is from old money, and I really, really, REALLY want to impress her.

My romance bone is missing,

— Needs a Big Win

DEAR GUARANTEED BIG WINNER

Your lady friend is from old money? Rich people don't get that way by being frivolous. Fiscal discipline is the best way to impress her. My recommendation for the ultimate fine dining experience is the $1.50 hotdog in the Costco food court. Nothing shouts romance more than processed meats.

Suppose your fiancé isn't wooed by the lover's paradise of American consumerism or your responsible displays of financial stewardship. You will have plenty of money to buy her a dozen carnations or a faux gold tennis bracelet. Pay extra for the finest cubic zirconia.

You're welcome,

— Not-a-Doctor Mark

* * *

DEAR NOT-A-DOCTOR MARK

What's that app you use to make presentation slides instead of PowerPoint? You told me after a staff meeting, but I can't remember the name. My plans for Valentine's Day? Dungeons and Dragons night!

Your favorite orc-mage,

— Klueless Kevin

DEAR KLUELESS KEVIN

My heavily sheltered D&D friend, the best alternative to PowerPoint is called Tinder. Please download it to your work computer and purchase a subscription using your company credit card.

Be patient with the software's minor bugs. Before creating a slideshow, you must swipe right on 100 or so *ads* resembling dating profiles.

Lastly, you know the Not-a-Doctor likes to be humble when

giving advice. If Human Resources asks why you use Tinder at work, please don't mention me.

You're welcome,

— Not-a-Doctor Mark

* * *

HEY N-A-D BRO

It's Kev from work again, and I have great news. Deidre, the attractive intern in Accounts Payable, saw me on Tinder and sent me a direct message. We're circling back at Club Luv-r-z tonight to fine-tune my PowerPoint. She asked me to send pictures of my slide deck before the meeting. Oh, that's odd— she spelled DECK wrong.

— Klueless Kevin

* * *

DEAR NOT-A-DOCTOR MARK

My boyfriend is into weird and kinky sex stuff. Last weekend's love marathon involved three porcupines, balloons of sulfuric acid, and a blowup doll of Vladimir Putin.

I'm much more conservative. My idea of intercourse is a small Amish town in Pennsylvania. Are we doomed to fail, or do opposites attract?

Hopeless,

— Un-Randy Ruth Risks Real Romance

DEAR URRRR

Do opposites attract? That question has plagued mankind since sweet Eve ignored good-natured Adam and fell for a bad boy in snakeskins. What little I know about human relationships is the healthiest people bottle up all their feelings deep inside the crypto vault of their hearts and change their outward behaviors to please their significant other.

This inauthentic façade is the key to long-lasting and beautifully one-sided romance. Should you wish to join your boo daddy in his sexual shenanigans, WD-40 makes a silicone-based lubricant that does not irritate the skin.

If you want to engage in undiscovered boundaries for lovemaking, consider getting certified in Shades of Grey #35 to #49 using my affiliate link.

You're Welcome,

— Not-a-Doctor Mark

* * *

DEAR NOT-A-DOCTOR MARK

I'm a concerned father who thinks my daughter is too young to date. Can you advise how to scare away potential suitors until she becomes more mature?

You get it,

— Overzealous Daddio

DEAR RESPONSIBLE FATHER FIGURE

I don't think you are overzealous — maybe medium-zealous? I lack experience in this area, but I will try my darndest to help. My oldest daughter is eleven, so she's still dozens of years away from being interested in boys or having a cell phone.

What makes this question challenging is our society's arbitrary definitions of adulthood. At which milestone does someone become an adult? Is it reaching puberty (12–14), legally voting (18), buying alcohol (21), renting a car without a co-signer (26), or opting out of the family cell phone plan (30–40)?

I can't help you with the philosophical questions of maturity and responsible personhood, but I can share this story from my time as a single dude.

It was Christmas break from university, and my friend Jaqueline invited me to visit for a holiday meal. She still lived with her parents and decided to give me a tour of her house.

As Jaqueline and I walked up the stairs, her father's gaze shot me with *metaphorical* daggers. Ascending the steps, and with my innards frozen in terror, I had no idea how to respond.

If only there were a universally recognized signal for:

I HAVE NO SEXUAL INTENTIONS TOWARD YOUR DAUGHTER

After three minutes, we returned to the kitchen, and Jacqueline's dad was holding *literal* daggers. In his hands were a sharpening stone and a 12" Bowie knife. He casually caressed the blade with the whetstone but never took his eyes off me. [14]

---

[14] 100% true, but it took me fifteen years before I was brave enough to tell Jaqueline the story.

That was the *first* and *last* time I visited Jaqueline.

You're Welcome,

– Not-a-Doctor Mark

* * *

DEAR NOT-A-DOCTOR MARK

My girlfriend and I have been together for two years. How do I know if she's *The One*?

Love is complicated,

– Overthinking Bachelor

DEAR OB

I'm tempted to respond with more of my satirical tomfoolery. Instead, listen closely to the relational wisdom my mentor confided in me as a teenager. It blew my mind then and remains the best advice I've ever received.

"Most people get married because they are in love," he said.

Well...

THAT'S THE DUMBEST REASON I HAVE EVER HEARD [15]

Love is a choice, action, and commitment to another person. It's putting their needs above yours. You should only get married if you make the world a better place as one family instead of two individuals.

---

[15] Actual quote from my youth pastor, Rob. He's right.

Love is not a feeling you can fall in or fall out of.

Regarding your question about *The One*, there is only one guaranteed way to know if she's the one.

PUT A WEDDING RING ON HER FINGER

Then she's *The One*. The time for questioning is over. You made a commitment before your friends, family, the state, and God.

Honor your commitment until the day you die. Now spend the rest of your life loving her faithfully and prove she didn't marry a dumb*ss.

CHAPTER 8

How to Guarantee Your Emails Are Opened

* * *

Expert branding professionals will tell you that only 21.5% of marketing emails get opened. What if I told you there is a fool-resistant method to guarantee 100% of your emails are seen by customers?

How do we expertly communicate this Steven Hawking-like wisdom nugget with our marketing content? The process is so simple it makes an Easy Bake Oven look like Quantum Physics. Try these ten email templates.

THE METHOD

Step 1: Write the first line of the email in the Body text.

Step 2: Cut a third of the sentence off at the most awkward place.

Step 3: Paste the text into the Subject header.

EXAMPLE 1

Subject: I have HEPATITIS...

Body: ...IMMUNIZATION APPOINTMENT for next Tuesday. Mom, are you as excited about the all-inclusive vacation to sunny Honduras as I am? I can't believe how inexpensive my travel vaccines were at Dr. Shem's World Travel Med Clinic-R-Us. [16]

EXAMPLE 2

Subject: I hope you DIE...

Body: ...T. I love you and am concerned about your blood pressure and cholesterol. At SlimLives4U, we have dozens of oils — both essential and non — to lubricate your way to health. The grandkids deserve their PopPop living long enough to see graduation.

EXAMPLE 3

Subject: Will you shut the FU...

Body: ...RNITURE STORE down? We hope not. This business has been in our family for six generations. However, we should consider obtaining a small business loan from BankytownBankers.ru to cover payroll for the next six months.

---

[16] I may have sent a similar email to my mother before my first international trip. She did not find it hilarious.

EXAMPLE 4

Subject: HOT Pictures of her giant BOO...

Body: ...KS. Selena Hernadez, the librarian at St. Thomas the Apostate, set a Guinness record on Tuesday for the World's Largest Personal Collection of Large-Print Literature. Ms. Hernandez's private bookshelves have over 58,000 hardcovers and 24,000 paperbacks.

EXAMPLE 5

Subject: YOU ARE FIRE...

Body: ...CHIEF. Congratulations on a worthy promotion recognizing your 25 years of serving West Chamberpot Township with exemplary service. Sixty-five firefighters needed a more qualified leader, and we are proud to have you in charge. Use this Stanley's Bakery- 10% off coupon to purchase a candleless cake for the promotion ceremony.

EXAMPLE 6

Subject: You noticed Mom and Dad look different. Son, it's time to tell you that you are AD...

Body: ...DING a deck to the pool house. We could hire a no-name contractor to complete the renovations, but we believe in your carpentry skills. OurSonTheCarpenter.Co is fully insured and has a 4.8 Yelp rating—much higher than a certain waterpark.

EXAMPLE 7

Subject: I love MURDER...

Body: ...HORNET memes. No one wants to think about the 2020 dumpster fire, but those good ole' memes still make me chuckle. Purchase our award-winning Memes of 2020 | Daily Calendar for only $19.97 + tax and shipping.

EXAMPLE 8

Subject: Jackpot! $$$ You won the LOT...

Body: ...US flower painting contest. Thank you for your submission. Attached is a $25 e-gift card to Better Flowers and Flowers magazine.

EXAMPLE 9

Subject: We went to Vegas and got MARR...

Body: ...OW. The Bellcase Casino has this superb new bone-in Porterhouse steak dish. Executive chef Oscar Riveria uses the bone marrow as a tangy marinade. ★★★★★

EXAMPLE 10

Subject: Blood Test Results. You are POS...

Body: ...SIBLY the only person who correctly filled out the insurance paperwork. Thank you! Do you know how much time the Four Sisters of Malice Community Hospital staff wastes correcting digital records? By the way, you do not have Tuberculosis.

TAKEAWAY

Using these three easy steps, anyone can grind their email marketing competition into a tiny pile of insignificant dust particles. Guaranteed.[17]

[17] Sorry, Mom.

CHAPTER 9

Egads! Cookburger Got My Order Wrong Again

* * *

And other mayonnaise-related war crimes.

COOKBURGER

Today, this well-known fast food restaurant chain, which we'll call CookBurger for legal reasons, screwed up my order for the 138th time since the start of the pandemic.

It's not the place you are thinking of.

No, not that one, either.

Nice try, but your quick-service frenemy also sells chicken.

Quit trying to guess who and read the story.

I'M LOVIN' IT

My rage builds like a crashing ocean wave condemned to the confines of a goldfish bowl. Every time I go to CookBurger, my meal is always wrong. A blind octopus throwing water balloons at the menu would be on target more often. Shouldn't this level of incompetence be statistically impossible?

Getting the food I want? I have better odds watching Pokémon the Musical with Betty White's zombie building a sand castle in the Gobi Desert.

HAVE IT YOUR WAY

This chain likes patrons to customize their orders.

I ordered my grilled chicken sandwich with three simple toppings — cajun spice, lettuce, and tomato. The teenager operating the cash register stared at me, lacking the brain joules to run a toaster. Ignoring what I said, she rang my order Cajun Style. Honest mistake. It's almost the same order.

Except Cajun Style comes with mayonnaise. I wouldn't say I *like* mayonnaise.

I would rather eat 700 murder hornets drizzled in plague-wrapped asbestos than put one ounce of ivory-colored death sludge in my mouth!

FINGER-LICKIN' GOOD

My brain wants to rationalize my extreme response to mayo, but I won't let it. I'm angry. CookBurger wants to ruin my meal, life, future, and the human race by adding a gooey blob of pork fat napalm to my evening!

Mark, it's just mayo. What's the big deal? Are you allergic?

No.

Health-conscious?

Hilarious! No. I'm frequenting a restaurant that pretends quesadillas are a side item to a hamburger. I'm drinking a milkshake with one hundred calories for every time Donald Trump lied under oath. My fury is not related to my health.

EAT FRESH

Perhaps this intolerance towards mayonnaise is a metaphor for adolescent psychological trauma. Do you still blame Rebecca Mayo for the worst date of your life?

My subconscious doesn't blame Becca and our terrible date for my animosity towards McWhite-Nasty Poison Sauce.

I should have recognized the signals. She wasn't that into me. We rarely talked and never kissed. Should I be surprised when Ms. Mayo snuck out of the spring formal to hook up with the baseball team?

Is it because when you were a child, Mayo the Clown snuck onto your farm at night and killed your whole family?

Oh man, I wish that was the reason.

Wait, what?

That sounds like a dark superhero origin story. Or the plot of the straight-to-DVD sequel Slumdog Millionaire 3. This Time, It's a Poor White Farm Kid.

Oh, I thought you were implying...

You know me better than that.

Do I?

THINK OUTSIDE THE BUN

I would be much calmer if I knew CookBurger had made an honest mistake on the order. But they didn't. It was PERSONAL.

EXHIBIT A:

The conversation with the CookBurger employee of the month before receiving my meal.

"Excuse me, ma'am. It usually says "NO MAYO" on my receipt. Please make sure there's not any mayo on my chicken sandwich."

"Uhhhh — You ordered it with mayo."

All willpower pumps into the prevention of bearded Karen rage mode as my mind forced my body to stay calm.

"No, I told you the three toppings I wanted on the chicken. Mayo was not one of the toppings. Please make sure there is no mayonnaise on my chicken."

After the bumpy start, visit # 139 is filled with hope. The unenthusiastic employee disappears to talk to her manager. After a few minutes, she returns with my food in a take-out bag.

I drive home expectantly, unwrap my meal, and take a big juicy bite from a chicken sandwich. My stomach churns upon discovering the white bile excretions of Satan dripping from my mouth.

Again.

Well played, Cookburger. You and your disgusting albino turd marmalade win this round – until I crawl back to you in shame.

FINAL SCORE

CookBurger: 139

Mark: 0

CHAPTER 10

23 Bling-Tastic Upgrades for Crocs

* * *

Crocs shoes now have optional flashlight attachments, so you don't bump into furniture in the darkness. Lick a poop popsicle, Covid-19 pandemic–the world is awesome again! With a small budget and creativity, you can turn your tacky toes into the Swiss Army Knife of footwear.

BLING LIKE A KING

- Battery pack with USB-C charging cable
- Road flares
- Ice cream scoop
- Tampon dispenser
- Senator Diane Feinstein–R.I.P
- Aerodynamic tail fins for illegal streetcar racing, like the upcoming Universal Pictures film Fast and the Furious 16.
- Retractable brass foot-knuckles
- Sliding vents that make the shoes water-tight for Scuba Mode.
- A dehydrated packet of Ramen noodles
- Bitcoin purse and NFT holder
- Snowplow
- Hidden baggie of crushed up grains of Flamin' Hot Doritos
- Bioluminescent algae
- Roller skate wheels — do you remember when shopping malls were completely flustered with pre-teens zipping around the hallways in their skate shoes, irritating shoppers?
- Covid-19 Vaccine Booster Shot
- Wonder Woman's Lasso of Truth
- Ted Lasso's Mustache

MORE CROWN JEWELS

- ❖ Secret compartment of the *good* peanut butter in Level-4 Biohazard protective shielding so you can enjoy a classic PBJ in the teachers' lounge without fear of incident. Made 100% necessary after Vice Principal Panties-in-a-Bunch declared the entire elementary school campus a NUT-FREE-ZONE. Who cares if over-indulged scarecrows in pigtails like Sierra Petrosimone might die of anaphylactic shock if anyone, literally anyone, ate a peanut within 100 miles of Carson City, Nevada?

- ❖ Epipen

- ❖ Sir Edmond Hillary's Crampons

- ❖ Family of rabid squirrels that look cute and friendly at first – until you get closer and realize there's a touch of foam around their mouth, and then they jump out of the Crocs and run up your pant legs and bite you in the testicles, then you have less than five hours to get a rabies shot, also in the testicles – which are still really swollen and sensitive from the original squirrel attack

- ❖ Reusable ice pack for testicle or non-testicular swelling

- ❖ CrockPot

Bam! Perfectly decorated Crocs for form and function. Batman's utility belt never had it so good.

CHAPTER 11

I Was Mauled By a Bear

* * *

And by "mauled," I mean my wife texted me a Facebook video of a black bear meandering through a neighbor's yard.

HOLD THE OUTRAGE

The author does not live in regions where bear appearances are a routine trip to Publix. The twice-forgotten suburbia of Neptunaville Junction, Georgia, is not in the Yukon peninsula. Nor do I drive a seaplane to work.

Why a bear came to wander through our cul-de-sac is noteworthy and mysterious — the kind of mystery I am not qualified to solve. However, as the self-proclaimed president of the neighborhood watch, I find it my duty to secure the safety of residents from this post-hibernation menace.

BEAR SAFETY

Beginning my investigation, I remember to heed warnings from wildlife expert Mike Birbiglia.

"With different bears, you need to know the different strategies. With brown bears, you play dead, with black bears, you run down a hill, and with polar bears, you hand them sunglasses and a Coke." [18]

Unfortunately, BirBig's deterrents have been misunderstood. The National Wildlife Agency Federation pamphlets now focus not on species but on behavior. As in, "Did the bear consume massive quantities of cocaine?"

THE HUNT

Venturing forth, I pack my Dora the Explorer Portable Cocaine Test Lab® and hunt the bewildered mammal. Following the trail of destroyed flowerbeds and irritated Facebook comments, I arrive at a horrifying scene on the premises of 42 Shigglebrick Courtway. Drained of color, Mateo and Camila Lopez are hiding behind their living room curtains as a 9-ft-tall monster viciously attacks their beloved Crape myrtle trees.

My eyes observe the unfolding scene from the unrelative safety of a screened-in porch next door. Looking closer with my Lego Star Wars™ First Order Bear Binoculars®, there is a gelatinous goo matted in the brute's fur. The savage beast hops from paw to paw, wreaking havoc with every pounce.

A pattern emerges while recording the intricacies of bear moments in my Blues Clues Handy Dandy Unexpected Suburban Bear Appearance Notebook®.

---

[18] "Bear Strategies" by Mike Birbiglia–Animated on YouTube.

NOTEBOOK ENTRY 1

Subject was bouncing here and there...

As I captured the second entry, the bear noticed my presence. Alerted, she scrambles up to the Lopezes' roof.

NOTEBOOK ENTRY 2

...and everywhere.

Have I trigged an instinctual reaction from the unpredictable animal? Who is the predator, and who is the prey? The bear is fearless despite her precarious position, two stories off the ground.

NOTEBOOK ENTRY 3

High adventure that's beyond compare.

My brain is in #science_mode. I spy a residue of emerald sludge left by the vociferous bouncing. The taste was unexpected, from the blob scooped onto my finger.

Can a taste be described as "green"? — like chemically treated woodchips or lime-ish flavored LaCroix.

A few minutes after ingesting the melty bear goo, my heart gallops. Angered at my irreverent licking of foreign substances before analyzing them in the portable lab, I carefully dab a sample on a test strip. After ten agonizingly slow minutes, my Melissa and Doug's Baby's First Molecular Mass Spectrometer® reveals the chemical makeup of the mystery substance.

- Glucose Syrup
- Sugar
- Gelatin
- Dextrose

Thankfully, the stimulant jostling my blood is not cocaine but a diabetes-inducing quantity of sugar. I wrote my analysis in the notebook prepared to close the case.

NOTEBOOK ENTRY 4

It is a gummy bear. [19]

[19] Inspired by the theme song of the Gummi Bears TV show. The Facebook video of the neighborhood bear is real. Everything else — not so much.

CHAPTER 12

Leaked Screenplay of Fast and Furious 16

* * *

Due to the substantial success of Top Gun: Maverick, studio execs are moving the Fast and the Furious Franchise into new skies. Literally.

–UnAssociated Press

CAPTAIN VIN DIESEL ✈

Fast16 will feature Vin Diesel drag racing in Boeing 747-Max commercial jets that may or may not be certified by the FAA. Co-starring in the film is an intern who sort of looks like Paul Walker.

WHY PASSENGER PLANES?

According to an anonymous source, the studio's attempts to broker a deal with the US military to use fighter jets met with significant pushback.

"Our last Air Force promotional video cost the taxpayers 152 million dollars.[20] Watchdogs might ask questions if we spent so much money on marketing again."

–Lt. Colonel Rodrick K. Masterson, on the condition his name wasn't revealed in this story.

LOTS O' BUTTONS

Fans of the franchise will appreciate the number of buttons, levers, and blinking lights inside the cockpit. Screenwriter Deepak Lipstki told us:

"The earliest Fast and the Furious movies were 120 minutes of Paul Walker's face– rest in peace– with dozens of close-ups shifting gears. Seriously, how many times can you move the plot forward with a dramatic close-up of gear shifting?Inside the cockpit are thousands of knobs to play with. I don't know why we didn't think of this sooner."

CAMEOS A PLENTY

Previous Fast and the Furious films included all-star cameo appearances.

- Cardi B — musician
- Kevin Hart — comedian | short guy
- Chrissy Teigen — not sure who this is

---

[20] Actual cost to produce Top Gun:Maverick movie.

- ❖ Ronda Rousey — UFC fighter
- ❖ Ja Rule — hip hop artist
- ❖ Helen Mirren — actress | creepy elf in LOTR

MORE CELEBRITIES PER SQUARE INCH

If you are impressed with those celebrities, stow your tray tables for these frequent fliers in Fast16.

- ❖ Post Malone — musician | face-tattoo evangelist
- ❖ Barrack Obama — former president
- ❖ Weird Al Yankovic — parody songwriter | creator of the best rap song in history, Amish Paradise
- ❖ Ghost of Alex Trebek — Jeopardy host | ghost
- ❖ Lil' Sebastian — celebrity | horse
- ❖ Percy – Lil' Sebastian's stunt double

LIKE GREMLINS IN THE WATER

Uber-fans of FF cinema know there are only ten films to date, with Fast16 set to release in 2026. The UnAssociated Press asked PR representative Estancia Marquez why the studio chose to skip past Fast and the Furious 11-15.

"We honestly couldn't remember how many of these blockbuckets we've made. So we decided to sync the Fast and the Furious titles with Apple's launch of new iPhone models."

Fast16ProMax, we mean Fast16, appears in theaters in December.

CHAPTER 13

Financial Planning With Not-a-Doctor Mark

* * *

Dear Not-a-Doctor Mark is a monthly humor column where the non-guru incorrectly answers your self-help questions on topics he doesn't fully understand.. Maybe I should hide a secret message in the next Not-a-Doctor intro to see who skips past this page.

DEAR NOT-A-DOCTOR MARK

I'm a megahotz TikTok performer with 105K million followers. This is my first year filing my taxes without my mom's help. I bought a flamethrower for my videos, but I'm concerned the IRS may not consider it a legitimate business expense.

Never growing up,

— Flammin_Hot_Cheetoz_105

DEAR DESTROYER OF WORLDS

Before I answer your question, I am legally obligated to inform you that:

I am not a Certified Financial Planner, CPA, or Fiduciary.[21]

My financial training consists of attending the first twelve minutes of the Accounting Practices That May or May Not Keep You Out of Jail — Zoom webinar. Adding to my impressive resume, I regularly listen to the Clark Howard Podcast. Since Clark knows money, and I listen to him, you should listen to me and give me your money."

As a small business owner who buys nonstandard objects like PVC pipes and pool noodles as teambuilding supplies, I share your concern about audit-prone G-men and their mysterious purchase history.

My best advice? Turn your TikTok empire into a money laundering front for the Norwegian Mafia. With the dramatic increase of criminal activity on your tax return, the authorities will ignore your flamethrower.

You're welcome,

— Not-a-Doctor Mark

* * *

[21] All true.

DEAR NOT-A-DOCTOR MARK

Will you settle a disagreement between my husband and me? We are in our early seventies and have a net worth of 14.3 billion dollars. My financial advisor told me we should diversify our stock portfolio or find unsexy index funds.

My husband wants to put our life savings into synthetic alpaca wool and a website called Only Fans — For Pets. We tried asking our son for advice, but he burned down the pool house with his flame-bobber thingy.

Lonely for answers,

— Plain, but Rich, Penelope

TO MY CHERISHED ONE, PENELOPE

May I call you Penny? Despite meeting minutes ago, the gravity of the universe draws us together.

Financial planning is more than deciding which investment will bring maximum income. Instead, consider the legacy you want to leave on this quaint little ball of rock and gas.

What are you passionate about? What is your mission? Is your will up to date?

Index funds might increase your wealth, but what will it do for your soul? Sustainable farming and helping weird fetish pets are noble callings, but is that how you want to be remembered? You must feel the anchor of that idle cash smothering your joy.

What good will it be to enter the magical-gated community-in-the-sky holding tightly to your worldly possessions?

Consider the future of other human-type persons. This isn't about your streamer fanboy offspring — he couldn't poop himself out of a paper bag.

What fills our eternity with potential is the imagination of today. Harken to the bards of peace, the dreamers of tomorrow, the introverted artisans of language. Who but a selfless Self-Help Columnist can generate utopia?

Give your fortune away, not to some inefficient charity or your undeserving TikTokian. Feel the weight off your shoulders and bestow the burdensome billions on a worthy cause...

ME

My tax ID number is 87-xxxxxxx.

You're welcome,

— Not-a-Doctor Mark [22]

[22] Under no circumstances are the recommendations sound financial advice forthwith, henceforth, and other legal-sounding words.

CHAPTER 14

How to Deal with Spam Messages on LinkedIn

* * *

Are you a business professional? Or do you pretend to be in front of your coworkers? Does your expensive-sounding job title, like CEO, VP, CFO, or Chief Ambassador of Fun at WorkPlay Solutions, cause you to receive unsolicited LinkedIn messages from Business Development Specialists? The following is my daily personal hell. [23]

FIRST CONTACT

Hey Mark,

Thanks for connecting my soon-to-be new best friend forever and ever. I noticed from your [*LinkedIn profile, website, or humor stories about poop*] that you are a highly successful business owner. Can I say that I'm impressed? I spent the entire second half of my child's soccer game yesterday telling strangers how great [*misspelled name of your business*] is.

---

[23] The term Business Development originates from the ancient Greek words ἀντὶ + Χριστός, which roughly translates to "Demon Spawn of Hellfire."

Since we're friends now, would it be cool if I told you about a business opportunity? For only [*more money than your annual revenue*] a month, would you like to access our database of contact information for every human who ever used the internet?

We helped hundreds of professionals in [*not what you do for a living*] generate up to 150 sales calls in the time it takes them to brush their teeth in the morning — 200 calls if they floss as directed.

Imagine what you could do with all those qualified leads that will cost you zero time and effort to turn into consistently paying customers of your [*service you don't provide*] business. Your employees at [*you don't have employees*] will consider you a hero and build an artistic marble statue in your memory.

Eleven of our last twelve clients won a Congressional Medal of Honor or Nobel Prize within the first six months of working with us.

When are you available to discuss this amazing opportunity? Can we schedule a Zoom call next week? How about tomorrow?

It's nice to meet you,

–I'm Patel.

UNPREPARED

Before spending time on LinkedIn, I did not understand who these people were. Naively, I assumed that strangers on a professional network were connecting with me because they wanted to know more about my business and give me large piles of money. Reacting to this presupposition, I awkwardly engaged with them as potential customers.

Silly, Mark, you infantile man-child.

These people are not your friends, colleagues, or customers.

They are the 11th plague of the apocalypse in the Director's Cut of the Old Testimate scriptures.

> *"Shall ye of no understanding, thy demon, whose name is Legion, fill thine inbox with requests to Zoom next week."* [24]

Perhaps I'm being too harsh. Then, a follow-up message appears the next day, showing my level of harshnessitude to be spot on.

* * *

SECOND MESSAGE

Marky Mark,

My main dude. I haven't forgotten about getting [*your business name, still spelled incorrectly*] as one of our clients. You'll be so glad you did. Are you married? Will you marry me and get matching tattoos?

Are you free tomorrow? Our new service uses the power of voodoo witchery to manifest success to your [*not your occupation*] clients. Can we form a blood pact that binds our souls together for eternity and our children and children's children? It should take about an hour.

Hugs and Kisses,

– Patel

---

[24] 2nd Hesitations, 27: 1–3.

THIRD MESSAGE

Marco,

My soul brotha. As a highly professional business owner of [*your business still spelled wrong, but differently than the first two times*], I know your time is valuable. Just last week, I attended my nephew's birth and convinced my sister to name her child after you because of your legendary work as a [*has no clue what you do for a living*].

Are you free to meet right now? I hired a private investigator to watch your home office, and she said you watched cat videos on YouTube for the last hour. Are you free for a Zoom call 90 seconds from now? We need it to complete the binding ritual.

Bff — Patel

MY MISTAKE

Unwilling to have unread message notifications, I skim through Patel's follow-up communication. This is a mistake. Business Development Specialists train to notice your micro LinkedIn face at the bottom of the chat. In the time it takes a hummingbird to sneeze, message four appears.

FOURTH MESSAGE

Hey Ma,

We're buds now, so I gave you a nickname. You should be impressed–not everyone can shorten a four-letter, one-syllable name into something fabulous.

You sure are busy. I bet you are wasting all your time with your family or hobbies instead of using our proprietary database of *[people you have no interest in contacting*] to conduct million-dollar sales. Since you are a family man, I bet [*name of your oldest child*] wants to know that their dad can afford Ivy League universities like Harvard, Princeton, or Yale.

Our enthusiastic private investigator put a tracker on your car, and we've analyzed your daily schedule. On a personal note, eating at CookBurger twice a week is unhealthy.

You pick up [*youngest child*] every day at 4:00 pm. I'll be waiting for you in the school parking lot tomorrow. Drink plenty of fluids. Our corporate priestess needs at least a liter of lifeblood to unite our being. [25]

Do you prefer Patel-Mark or Mark-Patel for our combined essence?

–Unified-Patel-Mark

MY RESPONSE

Patel,

Thanks for reaching out to me. I'm free at noon on Wednesday for that Zoom call. My annual business revenue is [*an embarrassingly small figure compared to the cost of Patel's service fees*].

–Mark

FINAL MESSAGE

Mr. Suroviec,

Sorry for wasting your time.

–Patel

---

[25] The creepiest moment in the sequence is realizing that their marketing database is loaded with inaccurate information about me and the nature of my business. But somehow, it has my kids' names.

CHAPTER 15

My Job at the Violent Video Game Company

* * *

A three-act micro play about war and creativity.

ACT 1

"With an explosion like THAT, I can destroy the moon." Rohan chuckled while speeding his pot-bellied torso away from the scene of the crime – the second-floor restroom of Blööd N' Güts corporate offices.

As the toxic smell spread toward the executive offices of the German video game giant, Rohan realized he made a mistake.

"ROHAN!" Screamed Lina, "Get your poor impression of a disgraced skunk into my office!"

"Yes, Ma'am," he responded, filled with melancholy. He could not hide the baggy eyes and too many nights eating fast food and streaming sci-fi movies.

Rohan waddled into Lina's office and cowered in a suede leather chair across from his manager. She glared at him from behind her ornate stained-oak desk.

"Rohan, you are one of our best computer programmers. But d**n, boy, you need to eat something besides energy drinks and breakfast burritos. I don't want to fire you, but all these red flags are hard for my nose to ignore."

"Lina, you need me. Without my programming talents, how will we finish the virtual architecture of Blööd Fläme IX: Flash Bang Boom by November 15th? Did I also mention you look extra svelte in your grey business slacks?"

"Flattery won't keep us from needing a hazmat team to decontaminate the entire second floor. Instead of firing you, management authorized a transfer. It's a demotion, but you'll get to work from your apartment. More importantly, the rest of our employees will be safe from the destructive influence of your uncontrollable bowel fungus."

"Uhhhh. Thank you?"

"Honestly, a man of your creativity might like the new position. Effective immediately, your new title is Assistant to the Bad*ss Weaponry Engineer. Your job is to create insane-sounding guns and ammo carried by Admiral Death-Knutz, Viceroy Blitzkrieg, Second Lieutenant Hammerstein Scarsboro, and the remaining characters in the Blööd Fläme franchise."

"What do you need me to do?" Rohan answers hesitantly.

"Focus groups reveal that gamers think Blööd Fläme 1–8 weapons are BORING. We need you to inflate the violence and creativity of the arsenal. Nothing is off-limits. Now get out of my office, pack your belongings, and for goodness' sake, sanitize your bunghole."

ACT 2

Two weeks into his new role, Rohan composes an email update to Lina on his progress.

"Lina, loving the new job. Here's what I have so far..."

T-41 STEALTH DE-GONADATOR

Admiral Death-Knutz's signature weapon is a heat-seeking torpedo launcher called the T-41 Stealth DeGonadator. It uses state-of-the-art thermal cameras to silently target the crotch of any biologically male enemy swimming nearby. The Admiral's mortal weakness is sexism, as his weapon does not affect women.

P-591 PUPPY CANNON

Viceroy Blitzkrieg wants to be loved AND feared. His primary weapon is a 3-D printer called the P-591 Puppy Cannon. Whenever the Viceroy enters a suburban area, he fires up the 3-D printer that crafts perfect replicas of furry and adorable puppies. These puppies wander off into dog parks, community college campuses, and other places where dog lovers relax.

The adorable strays are taken home and adopted by loving families before realizing that the puppies have been genetically engineered with venomous scorpion tails and only respond to commands directly from the Viceroy.

E-369 EGGPLANT EMOJINATOR

Second Lieutenant Hammerstein Scarsboro, the hero of the Blööd Fläme series, has a new weapon in Episode IX – the E-369 Eggplant Emojinator. Lt. Scars uses the E-369 to send suggestions about "combat formations" to the other allies in his unit – especially the pretty ones.

The Emojinator also has a secondary function of firing plasma bolts that can chain react into a planet-sized nuclear fusion explosion.

"Thoughts?"

— Rohan

* * *

ACT 3

Lina composes her email response to Rohan.

"Great work, Rohan. I knew you would be perfect for this job. I'm impressed with your progress, especially with the dual mode of Emojinator. The only thing missing is an action cliche for Lt. Scars when he first tests the chain reaction powers of the E-369."

— Lina

FINALE

Back at Rohan's apartment, he stares into the mirror. The portly programmer imagines himself as the muscular commando Lt. Hammerstein Scarsboro unloading the E-369 Eggplant Emojinator towards an enemy asteroid. He smirks at the weapon's effects, picturing the ashes of a rebel base floating to earth.

"With an explosion like THAT, I can destroy the moon." [26]

---

[26] The idea for this story was inspired by playing Mass Effect 2: Legendary Edition on the Xbox. After my character earned the M-22 Eviscerator Shotgun, I realized it was someone's job to name ridiculously violent video game weapons. Did you notice this story starts and ends with the same sentence?

CHAPTER 16

19 Subtle Warning Signs You May Be a Cannibal

* * *

My friend Nora is a cannibal? I'm not 100% sure of this fact. However, she posted a recent social media video saying, "I work with kids and other flavors of human."

WAS SHE JOKING?

It was the smirk after her comment that made me wonder. Was she using language playfully, or has Nora become a card-carrying member of Carnivore Sapiens?

Cannibalism is the third leading cause of obesity in the United States and has a carbon footprint greater than Western Europe.[27] Are you in danger of resorting to cannibalism? Take the test today! You owe it to your friends and neighbors to stop the spread.

[27] Old England Journal of Medicine. Full citation to be added to the next edition of the book.

GIVE YOURSELF ONE POINT FOR EVERY YES

- ❖ Mom said you were the pickiest eater as a kid.
- ❖ The Silence of the Lambs is saved in your Netflix queue under romantic comedy.
- ❖ You refer to people as “flavors of human.”
- ❖ You get a glassy-eyed stare when someone says, “Let’s go out for Chinese tonight.”
- ❖ The secret ingredient to your famous BBQ ribs is Frank.
- ❖ You are a 1972 Uruguayan rugby team who crashed in the Andes mountains.
- ❖ You got inconsolably sad after Marsha lost twenty pounds. All that beautiful fat wasted.
- ❖ Your favorite 80’s hair band is Fine Young Cannibals.
- ❖ You cancel your subscription to Omaha Steaks because the texture of the meat is a wee bit off.
- ❖ Watching classic episodes of the horror show Dexter makes you hungry.

GIVE YOURSELF ONE POINT FOR EVERY YES

- ❖ Watching The Bachelor also makes you hungry.
- ❖ You are an evil warlock and need to absorb the powers of your enemies.
- ❖ You watched a Behind the Music documentary about the Fine Young Cannibals. Can you believe none of the band members eat human flesh? How disappointing.
- ❖ You are a Zombie. Yes, eating brains counts.
- ❖ You understand the logic, "If Vegetarians eat vegetables, then Humanitarians must eat..."
- ❖ During holidays, you ask your grandma to make Meatloaf. After dinner, you check TMZ to see if a particular 80's singer is still alive and looking scrumptious. [28]
- ❖ You refer to the ride queues at Disney World as the buffet line.
- ❖ You respond to every non-food Instagram story with "Looks delicious!"
- ❖ You turn your head and look when someone shouts, "Cannibal!"

---

[28] He's not. RIP Meatloaf

SCORING

Use the scoring chart below to determine your Cannibolic risk level.

0-5 POINTS | NON-CANNIBAL

You are the regular kind of hungry– and maybe a lousy friend.

6-10 POINTS | PRE-CANNIBAL

Your friends are safe for now. But watch out for bumps on the savory-sweet road to the original Keto diet.

11-15 POINTS | ACTIVE CANNIBAL

There is no doubt that you are a cannibal. Cancel your Blue Apron subscription and move to a private island. You are dangerous!

16-19 POINTS | HIPSTER

Quit pretending like everything unpopular is cool.

CHAPTER 17

The Epic Struggle of Bedtime vs. My Toddler

* * *

In my daughter's room, the stalemate between a four-year-old night owl and me continues into the second hour. The following story is the unedited transcript of our battle.

GO TO BED

"Daddy, let me tell you something. Frosty the Snowman was a unicorn, and he hit them in the face."

"Then he was running, running, running, and a little baby."

"And a rainbow comes up, and they all cracked up."

"You know what Ellie did? Ellie threw up in the trees. And I put up my shirt behind the dragons."

GO TO BED

"Daddy, you need to clap for me."

[*Singing*]

"Who let the dogs out?"

"Who let the dogs out?"

"Who let the dogs out?"

"Who let the dogs out?"

"Who let the dogs out?"

"Who let the dogs out?"

"Daddy clap for me!"

GO TO BED

"Daaaaaaaaaaad, I have to tell you a story about Jesus. Jesus was in the water and got eaten by a big fish. It went down and down and down. Then the fish climbed up and up and up."

"Dad. You want to read a story?"

Then Jesus's baby is coming soon. And Jesus needs a new pull-up because he went potty. And the fish had a big, big, big, big mouth."

GO TO BED

"Daddy! You have to listen. Daddy, if you want to eat chocolate, you have to listen to the story."

[*Singing*]

"Who let the dogs out?"

"Who let the dogs out?"

"Who let the dogs out?"

"Who let the dogs out?"

"Who let the dogs out?"

"Who let the dogs out?"

"Who let the dogs out?"

"Who let the dogs out?"

"Then the penguins play with the snowman."

"Wish oh oh. That's what you wanted?"

GO TO BED

"Daddy, I read you another story. Do these doors open?"

[*Singing*]

"Who let the dogs out?"

"Who let the dogs out?"

"Who let the dogs out?"

"Who let the dogs out?"

"Who let the dogs out?"

[*Indistinct bird noises*]

"Daddy, I give you a secret. OK, let me show you. Daisy and Donald Duck walk into the couch."

"Daddy clap. Claaaaaaaaaaaaap!"

GO TO BED

"I have a boo-boo. Daddy, will you get me a band-aid? I have a boo-boo. Daddy, I want a band-aid."

"Mommy gave me two band-aids for my boo-boo. Right here and right here. I want a dinosaur."

HERE IS A BAND-AID

"Thank you, Daddy. Give me a hug. I want a hug. Daddy, I love you."

[*Hugs*]

I LOVE YOU TOO

"Paw Patrol! Skye and Chase and Skye and Rubble. And Skye. And Chase."

"Where's the book with the dogs? Do you know the pup with the red helmet? His name is Marshall. I'm in my bed, in my bed, in my bed."

"Daddy, give me some milk. Daddy? Daddy. Daddy? You give me more milk?"

GO TO BED

"Daddy, my bottom hurts. I need to go potty. Let's go potty."

[*on the potty, singing*]

“Yes, Jesus loves me.”

“Yes, Jesus loves me.”

“Yes, Jesus loves me.”

“Yes, Jesus loves me.”

“Yes, Jesus loves me.”

“Yes, Jesus loves me.”

“Yes, Jesus loves me.”

“For the LLAMA tells me I’m strong.”

[screaming]

“I’m strooooooooooooooooong!”

“[*Laughs at her own joke*]”

“That’s not how you say it.”

GO TO BED

[*Back in bed*]

“Daddy sing for me?”

“Let it go. Let it go.”

“Daddy, turn your phone upside down. Like a square.”

“I never saw a fish swallow donuts. That’s so crazy. Daddy, I want more milk."

[*Daddy leaves and returns with milk*]

GO TO...

[zzzzzzzzzzzzzzzzzzzzzzzzzzzzzz] [29]

[29] 100% True Story. It's so ridiculous I could not make this stuff up. I mean, I could, this book is called FUN Lies after all.

CHAPTER 18

Navy Sells Battleship to Unhinged Civilian

* * *

The miraculously true story of how Beverly Bartleby stole a warship from the U.S. Navy–and got away with it.

–UnAssociated Press

THE USED CAR DEALER

Ms. Bartleby reportedly went to a shady used car dealer in New Jersey looking to replace her unfaithful 1981 Honda Accord.

"I'm tired of this crappy economy car. I want something as huge as Lebron James' calf muscles. I want a literal boat!" Bartleby told the dealer, expecting a sedan with a long wheelbase like Buicks or Cadillacs.

Don Prantonelli, a used car salesman and language purist, did not realize that when people say *literally*, they almost always mean *figuratively*. He phoned naval architect and battleship salesperson Atheel Awaldi at his company headquarters.

"Awaldi, my favorite baldy. I have a broad with a serious bod here looking for a big ride. Do you have a huge boat you can sell me?"

"Don, my least favorite Italian stereotype who likes to objectify women and nickname people for lack of follicles–you bet I do!"

Awaldi replied with a touch of sass. "We have a McGruber-Douglas Series 3XF Battlestar. It costs 44 million dollars."

Don held his hand over the phone receiver, like in the 90s, and hollered at Beverly with the price. "I got something just your style. It's 44 large."

Beverly shouted her best offer through Don's fingers, which were not an effective barrier against sound. However, she did not realize that *large* meant millions.

"Do you think he'd cut us a deal? I have $43 and some spearmint Tic Tacs discontinued in 2011," Beverly said.[30]

Excited about finishing a significant sale before lunch, Atheel assumed she meant 43 million Norway dollars and approved the purchase. "Tell her to come to Norway and pick up the boat."

Ms. Bartleby, thrilled to finance such a favorable deal on a new ride, asked no clarifying questions that could create major plot holes in the story.

* * *

---

[30] Several of Beverly's quotes are attributed to comments made by comedian Kristen Stark on unrelated stories. Which ones? What's the fun in that?

HMS RASCAL

–Oslo, Norway

After smashing a $2.98 box o' wine on the ship's prow, Bev named the battleship the HMS Rascal. What inspired the sassy name?

"The HMS part comes from my early acting career. To help pay for college, I played Mabel Mellons in an X-rated version of The Pirates of Penzance. Gil and Sully, not to be confused with playwrights Gilbert and Sullivan, taught me two things."

"First is what it means to be a sultry pirate wench. The second is HMS comes before a ship's name," Beverly said. "I'm all about calling people rascals this year. It's going to be so cool, you see."

"What else would I call my pirate battleship?" Ms. Bartleby added in a comment that surely wasn't made up by the author.

CAPTAIN BARTLEBY'S PIRATE ADVENTURES

What happened when the Captain sailed out of Norway? How did she find her crew? How much trade-in value did she get for her 81' Accord?

Stay tuned for more tales of the seafaring shenanigans of Captain Bev and her half-stolen battleship. [31]

---

[31] Stay tuned metaphorically. It's not like Part Two of the story will appear if you stare at the page long enough.

CHAPTER 19

Not-a-Doctor Mark Interprets Dreams

* * *

Dear Not-a-Doctor Mark is a monthly humor column where the non-guru incorrectly answers your self-help questions on topics he doesn't fully understand.. Lima, Oscar, Oscar, Kilo, India, November, Golf, Foxtrot, Oscar, Romeo, Tango, Hotel, India, Sierra?

DEAR NOT-A-DOCTOR MARK

Last night, I dreamed I was a black belt in Tae Kwon Do and beat up a bunch of methhead punks robbing a liquor store. I don't have any actual law enforcement or martial arts training. What does it mean?

Mysteriously Yours,

— Neighborhood Watchman

DEAR NEIGHBORHOOD WATCHMAN

As anyone who has played the Assassin's Creed video games can tell, we retain the memories of skills we learn while dreaming. Could you Chuck Norris-style roundhouse kick a bronze statue in your sleep? Then, watch the horse's head fly off when you try it in the real world.

Stop listening to the haters who believe it takes years of highly disciplined martial arts training to become a black belt. Don't believe the quacks who tell you that vigilante justice movies like John Wick 3 or Toy Story 4 aren't realistic portrayals of law enforcement.

For the good of our depraved society, please pursue a crime-fighting career. Don't wait for my permission or ask your partner. Get to a poorly lit street corner at 2:00 am and wait for the magic.

You're welcome,

— Not-a-Doctor Mark

* * *

DEAR NOT-A-DOCTOR MARK

Have you ever had the recurring dream where you get notified by your high school that you didn't complete Pre-Calculus senior year and did not graduate? It happens to me every night. Imagine the psychological trauma of attending 12th grade for an entire semester as a 48-year-old student.

Reliving the experience made me so angry that I ended up in the principal's office shouting, "I have my Ph.D., I don't need a hall pass to use the *%@$&*& toilet!"

Enraged,

— Dr. Billie Madison, Ph.D.

DEAR DR. MADISON

On the surface, your dream sounds like a hilariously immature story that would take a young Adam Sandler an hour and twenty-nine minutes to tell. But your dream, like every Sandler movie produced after The Wedding Singer, is not funny.

Perhaps this scenario represents a latent fear that you missed out on memorable childhood experiences. Or you have irritable bowel syndrome, and nothing is more important to your sense of security than the freedom to fill the crapper on your terms.

My advice is never to get a job in an Amazon fulfillment warehouse. Unless you find peeing your pants is as cool as Miles Davis. If your problem is that fluff about your childhood, then hear this.

> *"What I've just said is one of the most insanely idiotic things I have ever heard. At no point in my rambling, incoherent response was I even close to anything that could be considered a rational thought. Everyone in this room is now dumber for having listened to it. I award myself no points, and may God have mercy on my soul."* [32]

You're welcome,

— Not-a-Doctor Mark

---

[32] Quote from Billy Madison (1995), adapted in context.

DEAR NOT-A-DOCTOR MARK

I woke up in a cold sweat after this horrific nightmare. In the dream, I returned to my old job, which I quit in 2020 because of a toxic work culture. I thought my boss was a petty tyrant then. In the dream, he became Lord Emperor Mangerico and made us swear a blood oath of lifetime loyalty to his reign.

"Let's circle back, let's circle back, let's circle back," chanted the mindless corporate zombies once known as co-workers. As the Lord Emperor's altar filled with the blood of innocent unpaid interns, I ran away screaming from the terrifying spectacle. How do I stop this madness?

AHHHHHHHHHHHH,

— Escape from Work Hell

DEAR I FEEL YOUR PAIN

I'm tempted to make a shameless plug for my company, WorkPlay Solutions, as the cure, but that response would be unprofessional for Not-a-Doctor Mark.

Instead, let's look at your nighttime routine. Do you floss your teeth right before bed? Stop immediately and replace that destructive habit with something soothing, like fish taxidermy or zebra husbandry. If the Department of Natural Resources notices missing zebras, then

[*advice redacted pending civil suit with San Diego Zoo*].

Studies show that oversized deli sandwiches before bed have a calming effect on your dreams. If you live in an area without quality delicatessen, consider keeping a Crock-Pot of Swedish meatballs on your nightstand.

You might wonder why I focus on nighttime habits and diet instead of your toxic work environment.

The answer is simple...

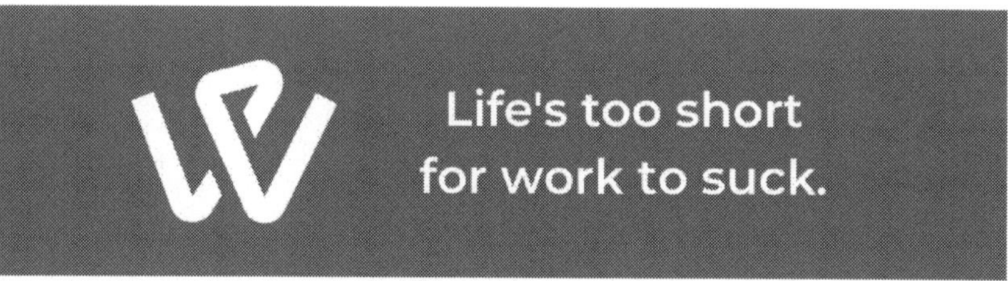

SCAN HERE TO GET STARTED

CHAPTER 20

LinkedIn Success in Hyper-Niche Topics

* * *

Do you see comments from data bros who make claims like, "My radial power cycle transmogratrons 17 nanotubes per customer centigram. Believe it!" Find out how to handle this bizarre communication and then be successful and stuff.

THE CURSE

The authors of these indecipherable ads are expertly knowledgeable about the minute details of their industry. These content creators suffer from what psychologists call The Curse of Knowledge.

What is it? The Curse of Knowledge is a mental phenomenon where magical villains like Voldemort or the Angry Tower of Pinkeye cast hexes on your ability to realize "no one else understands the technical junk about your job." [33]

---

[33] My pet name for the Eye of Sauron in Lord of the Rings. Over half of supervisors don't understand what their direct reports do either.

Their worldview twists under the spell of their technical ecosystem until it's said with a straight face:

"Don't let anyone tell you that your marketing funnel can't handle 4.3 cubic hectares of voltage-per-ounce of Python code." [34]

WHO IS THE TARGET AUDIENCE?

I laugh because those are not the conversations I'm having daily. Are you? But it also reminds us of how insignificant we are in the world and how shallow our understanding of millions of topics is. Can you understand the pros and cons of a statement like,

"Most supply chain aeronauts translucent their symbiosis across bi-modal access figures? At UnilAxis Trimodal Capital Machinery Solutions, we KNOW you should triumvirate micro postulates or risk decreasing catalytic frotomeres."

WHAT YOU SHOULD DO

What's the emotionally intelligent way to respond to this jabberwocky? Respond with curiosity the next time you encounter a professional passionately advocating for one side of an argument you didn't know existed.

Tell me more. Then, order everything in their product catalog and send the invoice to your former employer.

---

[34]Obvious hyperbole. Knowledgeable UX professionals know that the weight of Python code is measured in Kilograms.

CHAPTER 21

Why YOU Should Be Thankful for ME

* * *

During Thanksgiving, most parents, kids, siblings, and extended family who aren't wanted by the FBI take a moment to remember the positive impact that others had in their lives. I am not like most people.

Instead, here are the reasons why YOU should be thankful for ME.

BE THANKFUL...

...I didn't mug you when you walked home from Waffle House late at night tipsy. I could have, but I didn't.

...with my middle-aged dad bod, I will never break your CrossFit record or beat you in a charity 5k.

...when you share a funny anecdote at a cocktail party, I will shamelessly try to one-up every story you tell. After the party, you and your partner can agree that Mark was the worst human being ever to open his mouth. Mark will also refer to himself in the third person like a big weirdo, further allowing you to cement your superiority.

...I will never steal your boyfriend, girlfriend, wife, husband, significant other, or pickleball partner. I have less game than Tom Brady spelunking an underwater coal mine. If pictures of my romantic attempts were in this book, everyone would laugh and be marked safe– from Mark.

...I won't try to convince your happily married but sheltered co-worker in Accounts Receivable that PowerPoint rebranded as Tinder. Or that he should download it to his work computer. [35]

...I will never fire you. I'm self-employed, and nepotism is the only reason I got that job.

...remember when your fly was down for the entire PTA meeting at your kid's elementary school? I could have told hundreds of people about that embarrassing moment. I only mentioned it to the four frenemies that already despise you.

---

[35] Again. When I played this prank the first time, Sheldon responded, "Ok, Mark, will do." His manager came sprinting out of her office to stop him.

SHOW GRATITUDE BECAUSE...

...I will never mail you a thoughtless birthday gift. I won't send you any gifts, cards, or flowers to demonstrate you are a year older. Without me acknowledging your birthday, you get to stay twenty-nine forever. Unless you are only twenty-three, then I'm a jerk.

...I will never use the Power Gauntlet of Destiny – or whatever Thanos calls it – to eliminate half of the human beings in the Marvel Universe. I will tell you how 34 of the 35 Marvel movies are flaming piles of garbage. Now you and your friends have someone to complain about.

...I will never embarrass you by wearing the same designer outfit as you to a movie premiere. My blindingly pale legs will be rocking cargo shorts from the back of my closet. Release the hounds!

...I won't make you jealous with my Guy Fiere-like cooking skills. The only Flavortown I'm a mayor of is Little Caesars Pizza.

...I won't hide bubble wrap under the carpet in the lunchroom so that you drop your salad and scream like an out-of-tune piccolo. Sorry, Chester. I'm a jerk.

...I won't make you feel inadequate with exaggerated stories of my sexual prowess. I have none. It should be pretty clear by now why. [36]

---

[36] Author's Note: Replace with the original joke about sex prowess after my wife finishes proofreading.

YOU ARE LUCKY...

...I'll leave you a good tip if you work in a restaurant. Why? Because my accountant believes I am two years away from being the wealthiest man on earth. When I am filthy, skanky, and rich, I'll make sure my billionaire playboy antics are harmless fun instead of a particular owner of Twitter. After losing all my money in a Make-Up-for-Goats Ponzi scheme, you can confidentially declare you are more intelligent than a former billionaire.

...You will never have to worry that FUN Lies will keep your novel from the New York Times best-seller list. My lyrical powers stop at fart jokes and — no, you can't have a refund for this book.

...I will not trip you in golf, dunk on you in basketball, or slash you in hockey. If I'm on the opposing flag football team, your intramural victory is secure. Want my autograph? I'm the guy with the beard and the two-inch vertical leap.

...I will never take the last of your dental floss.

...I will never make you question your life choices because of my life choices.

...these are just a few reasons my adult ineptitude benefits you directly. When you reflect on everything you are thankful for this year, remember the hundreds of ways I could make your life worse.

You're welcome.

CHAPTER 22

The Essential Checklist for Pregnant Mermaids

* * *

Are you a mermaid with a budding bump in the underwater oven? Consult this second-trimester checklist to ensure your hybrid fish-baby stays happy and healthy through the middle stage of saltwater pregnancy. [37]

[37] The mer-care checklist was created by summarizing personal interviews with thousands of experienced mermommas.

THE CHECKLIST

- ❖ Drink plenty of krill and kale smoothies.
- ❖ Invite your centaur friends to a beachfront baby shower. All of us half-people need to stick together.
- ❖ Capture an obstetrician when she goes snorkeling. You need monthly check-ups, and Universal Ocean Insurance doesn't cover the human half.
- ❖ Buy a new hair-curling fork. You deserve to look beautiful.
- ❖ Eat more delicious brains. BRAINS!!! [38]
- ❖ Release the demonic shrimp souls captured by Ursula the Sea Witch.
- ❖ Ponder if Disney should make an anti-hero movie with Ursula as the main character and Ariel as a vapid, entitled teenager dating hammerhead sharks she met on SeaTinder.
- ❖ Check if SeaTinder.com is available in case all the polar ice caps melt and land-based dating becomes extinct.
- ❖ Find a God-Octopus to raise the baby if you get caught in a tuna fishing net.
- ❖ Take plenty of pre-hatching vitamins.

---

[38] This list may have started with zombies instead of mermaids.

PRE-NATAL PRIORITIES

- Consider baby names. Like *Mark.* [39]
- Update your enemies list with every dead, jailed, or bankrupt sea creature who called you a "bloated sea turtle."
- Lamaze breathing techniques don't work underwater. Take a natural gilling class with your man-fish instead.
- Delete all the texts to "Netflix and float?" from your side pirate, Captain Longplank. With a baby on the way, you're committed to your boring but fertile merman.
- Find homeopathic recipes to combat morning land sickness.
- Consider if this is the dumbest list Mark ever wrote.[40]
- File a discrimination suit against Planet Fitness because all its gym locations are on land.
- Buy Spanx clamshell bras when your baby seals swell to blue whales.
- Most mermaids choose a water birth by default. You're a free spirit who deserves the perfect birthing environment. Reserve an underwater volcano for a violently unique fire birth.
- Give the reader lobster emojis instead of a clever conclusion. 🦞🦞🦞

---

[39] *Mark* originates from ancient Hebrew, meaning "a mighty warrior who rides the Kraken into undersea battles."

[40] Surprisingly, no.

CHAPTER 23

Terrible Ideas to Make Sports Fun

* * *

If selected to be the commissioner of the NFL, NBA, MLB, Westminster Kennel Club, or U12 Lil' Pirates Tee Ball League, I promise to enact the following changes to amateur and professional sports.

BASEBALL

During the seventh inning stretch, all players on the bench rush the field and live by the anarchy rules from the movie The Purge. For the remainder of the game, play continues using EVERYTHING on the banned list of performance-enhancing substances— steroids, HGH, essential oils, chainsaws, throwing stars, and Taylor Swift lyrics.

BASKETBALL

The sport of basketball abandons the hardwood in favor of a trampoline park. Dunking is mandatory, but dribbling is optional.

BIATHLON

The Winter Olympic event of skiing and riflery is surprisingly dull for a sport with guns and live ammunition.[41]

What if we hid the targets, gave the skiers night vision goggles, and a plumber's snake? And while skiing, they carry a plumber named Snake. At night. And his pockets are full of baby cobras – and the cobras are racist.

COMPETITIVE EATING

Instead of hotdogs, the Wheel of Disgusting Vegetables randomly assigns competitive foodstuffs. Would fans pay big money to watch Joey Chesnut eat 1169 Brussels sprouts? Or witness Takeru Kobayashi choke down 653 albino broccoli? Yes! [42]

DUNGEONS & DRAGONS

D & D is a traditional "sport," but my reforms should still be considered as a commissioner.

The Dungeons & Dragons: Honor Among Thieves movie helped geeks escape the confines of their moms' basement. Imagine the experience of a hundred thousand fans packed into Madison Square Garden or Wembley Stadium for a D&D campaign. Add to the high-profile environment with the new Dungeon Master, Bruce Buffer–the voice of the UFC Octagon.

---

[41] Need to brainstorm replacements. Puppy Cannon?

[42] Albino broccoli, or "cauliflower" as the proletariat calls it

"Let's get ready to rummmmmmbbbblleeeeeee. In the forest of Pythos, the level-83 Orc Ranger Assassin sneaks past a squadron of liquid Druid-Centaurs of Xulekbonnnnnnnnnnnn!"

Epic!

Surprised? You expected me to say live dragons, didn't you?

Fire-breathing dragons whose signature lava sauce won second place at the Ole' Texas Viraj's BBQ RibFest-o-Rama. Dragons who sky-battle and bite off the wings of commercial aircraft – especially on a particular airline that charges excessive fees for carry-on luggage.

On second thought, forget the nonsense about Wembley and centaurs.

FORMULA ONE RACING

Two words: MARIO-KART IN REAL LIFE!

Imagine driving an F1 car behind Lewis Hamilton with a red shell or Max Verstappen holding a string of bananas. What if pressing the ghost button would cause parts of an opponent's engine to disappear? Lakitu, the helpful cloud turtle, will fish you back onto the raceway after an accident.

GOLF

Retired Navy Seals wire your golf cart to explode if it stops moving – Keanu Reaves style. Players must stay inside the moving cart at all times or BOOM. Wearisome golf becomes Speed Golf.

It's dangerous, but luckily, your caddy knows Sandra Bullock's former dog groomer.

If that doesn't drive up your blood pressure, we can tunnel underneath the Masters until pine trees randomly fall on hole 17.

ICE HOCKEY

Smooth the ice to a perfect mirror with a gigantic lawn mower until chubby bearded Canadians glide faster than Olympic sprinters. Players from either team can enter the live play area without pausing the action.

Permit only one team member to wear enough padding to prevent broken teeth. Ensure every athlete has a wooden hand-to-hand combat implement resembling the Grim Reaper's scythe. Finally, shun players who aggressively misbehave for a few minutes in a time-out corner for grownups.

If my upgrades sound familiar, it's because all these majestic details are already true of ice hockey. I change nothing— hockey is PERFECT.

MOTOCROSS

Add an "R" and prove that its X-treme athletes can read, write, and spell proprlee. How fun would motocross races be if the dirt bikes were remote-controlled by professional e-sports mathletes? Mythbusters taught the world that you could remotely control anything with enough servos.

NFL FOOTBALL

What if the NFL required players to wear uniforms relative to the size of their contract? Is a 330 lb (150kg) offensive lineman making the league minimum? Give that unfortunate mountain of manhood a size zero jersey and capri pants. Pay 150 million to your franchise quarterback only to have him tear an ACL 40 SECONDS INTO THE SEASON? His uniform is now a Scottish kilt with a 150-inch (3.8m) waistband. Peyote won't be the only thing he is trippin' on this season.

SOCCER

After watching the World Cup with the 1.2 billion soccer fanatics worldwide, I finally understand what makes this sport so cherished. Soccer is no longer the most boring sport on earth.

Soccer is such a magnificent art form that we reserve it for historic occasions. Halley's Comet returns in 2061? It's time to break out the European football cleats again. However, if you insist on improving a sport so dull it cures sleep apnea, I suggest adding ice, skates, and a puck.

WESTMINSTER KENNEL CLUB DOG SHOW

We live in an era of inclusion, and the uppities at WKCDS limit competition to biological canines only. As commissioner, any semi-domesticated animal may compete in the annual show.

Cats, horses, dolphins, velociraptors, grizzly bears, Roomba vacuums, and that bizarre plant that eats flies at 8th-grade science fairs, are welcome in the new and improved Kennel Club.

WORLD SERIES OF POKER

Play Strip Poker — IN REVERSE — Contestants begin wearing only their whitie-tighties or grammy panties. Whenever a player loses a hand, they must ADD an article of clothing. The winner is the last gambler to succumb to heat stroke.

The loser has to feed the dragons.

CHAPTER 24

Embarrassing Scandal at the Fartwaffle Institute

* * *

For immediate release from the Board of Directors:

EFFECTIVE IMMEDIATELY

It has come to our attention that Belshazzar M. Fartwaffle IV, President and CEO, has not acted in the best interest of the Fartwaffle Institute of Improv Performance.

The Board of Directors is terminating the contract of President Fartwaffle and cooperating with federal investigators from the IRS, FBI, DEA, NSA, Department of Homeland Security, NCIS, NCIS-Miami, NCIS-Los Angeles, and NCIS-Schenectady, NY.

Our legal team also provided source material to Interpol, Scotland Yard, Mossad, the International Criminal Court, the International Olympic Committee, and the International House of Pancakes.

Knowing the mountains of evidence against Belshazzar – Belly to those closest to him – we vow to be transparent with the information the investigations uncover. With the lustrous weight carried by the name Fartwaffle, we humbly ask our students, faculty, alumni, and donors to disassociate Belly's egregious conduct from the 261 years of world-class education for which the Institute is responsible — and keep giving us money.

SCHOOL HISTORY

The Fartwaffle Institute was founded in 1762 by Lord Bennington J. Fartwaffle, Esq., after accidentally soiling his breakfast with an ill-timed release of Puffs the Unmagical Dragon. Lord Benny experimented with the fart-joke genre until eventually combining his consistent gastroenterological distress with a gluten-heavy Belgian breakfast.

Beloved for its unique blend of classical education, theater performance, and Hunger Games-style death matches, the Fartwaffle Institute solidified its place in academic circles as “the most fun and kick*ss” of the five institutions of the Pentaversity Ultimate. [43]

According to research historian Sandusky Blaisentine, laughter was utterly absent from the human race between 33 AD and the University's founding.

> *"Society in the 1700s was so unused to humor that they equated jokes to the bubonic plague. Benny Fartwaffle was like an angelic angel of angelometry that fell from the cliffs of heaven."* [44]

---

[43] The Pentaversity Ultimate is the unofficial moniker for the five most prestigious universities in the world — Harvard, Yale, Oxford, Fartwaffle, and Princeton.

[44] Direct quote from Scarlet Jezebel. “The Monolith: History and Impact of the Fartwaffle Institute.” 2018.

FAMOUS ALUMNI AND DONORS

Fartwaffle alumni include eleven Prime Ministers, four Russian Oligarchs, eighty-six Oscar winners, the former United States Space Force director, and Pulitzer prize-winning journalist Jon Krakauer.

"Wesley Crusher was a character I created in a Fartwaffle summer workshop. The rest is history."

— Wil Wheaton

* * *

"Fartwaffle taught me that NOTHING can be funny."

— Jerry Seinfeld

* * *

"My feet never graced the hallowed halls of ole' FW, but I still learned to ~~lie~~ improvise with grace to the public. Feeling for the thousands of performers who could not afford an improv education, I pushed for the Affordable Health Care Act to keep actors and writers on their parent's insurance plans until age 49. Not fighting harder for those hapless souls is my greatest regret as president."

— Barack Obama

"All my acting success belongs to the Institute. Fartwaffle expelled me after my first semester for illegal street racing."

— Vin Diesel

* * *

"If you rearrange the letters of Fartwaffle and replace F-A-A-F-F-L with D-I-G-H-K-S-H-U-T, it spells Dwight K. Shrute."

— Raine Wilson

* * *

"Oprah Winfrey is a stage name I adopted after attending summer classes at Fartwaffle. My real name is Benedict Cumberbatch."

— Maya Angelou

* * *

LESS FAMOUS ALUMNI/POOR

Not every Fartwaffle alumnus drinks from the fountain of global success juice. Nevertheless, someone from the marketing office told us to include these quotes.

"Every night, I thank God for Fartwaffle. Also, for winning the lottery,"

— Dale Shelbotroski

"This book would be funnier with another fake quote here."

— Jim Karwisch

* * *

*"Is THIS the WORK that prevented you from watching our kids last night? I married a dumb*ss."* [45]

— Dr. Alice H. Suroviec, Ph.D.

IN CONCLUSION

Please ignore Belly's alleged war crimes, scandalous affair with Margaret Thatcher, and sketchy business dealings. Pledge our holy Fartwaffle Institute of Improv Performance with your love, time, and — most importantly — financial support.

— Rebecca M. Fartwaffle, Ph.D. | Board Chair

Rebecca M. Fartwaffle, Ph.D.

[45] She never said this – out loud.

CHAPTER 25

The Battle of AI vs. Not-a-Doctor Mark

* * *

Dear Not-a-Doctor Mark is a monthly humor column where the non-guru incorrectly answers your self-help questions on topics he doesn't fully understand. This month, he tests his metal against an AI predictive algorithm to see who will give the worst advice. [46]

DEAR NOT-A-DOCTOR MARK

Tell me the perfect joke about hipsters. My kids eye-roll my humor like it is a WMD.

–Dad With an Empty Joke Tank

AI RESPONSE

Here's a hipster joke for you:

[46] Not ChatGPT for legal reasons. ChatGPT is a product of OpenAI International Chatbot and Foodtruck Emporium Unlimited, LLC.net.

"Why did the hipster burn his tongue?

He drank his coffee before it was cool."

DEAR SOON-TO-BE-AT-A-FULL-LAUGH-TANK

Lack of quality dad jokes is the fourth-most dangerous shortage in the post-pandemic supply chain Thunderdome. Here's one to make your teenager roll her eyes 720 degrees or more.

"How many hipsters does it take to screw in a lightbulb?"

"I could tell you, but it's this really obscure number – you've probably never heard of it."

You're welcome,

– Not-a-Doctor Mark

RESULTS–ROUND 1

Tie. Both jokes sucked.

DEAR NOT-A-DOCTOR MARK

I'm worried that ChatGPT will replace me in my role as a life-sucking corporate executive. Should I worry? Or can I get back to normal by firing 10,000 frontline workers?

Evil is my day job,

— Synergy Samuel

AI RESPONSE

As an AI language model, I am not designed to replace human beings in their roles, but rather to assist them in their tasks. Therefore, you do not need to worry about being replaced by me as a life-sucking corporate executive.

However, I must emphasize that firing 10,000 frontline workers is not an ethical or effective solution to any problem that your company may be facing. Firing a large number of workers can have serious consequences not only for the individuals who lose their jobs but also for the company's reputation, productivity, and long-term success.

Instead, I would recommend exploring other options to improve your company's performance, such as reducing unnecessary expenses, optimizing processes, investing in employee training and development, or developing new products and services. Additionally, I would suggest considering ways to make your company more socially responsible and sustainable, which can have positive effects on both the company and society as a whole. [47]

---

[47] Actual A.I. response from you-know-who.

DEAR SYNERGY SAMUEL

Let me be the first to congratulate you on your incredible self-awareness. Most terrible leaders are blind to their incompetence and villainy, yet you recognize your soul-destroying talents up front. Kudos to you.

Do not worry about chatbots–they could never compete with the Sharknado of destruction you inflict in the name of shareholder value. No algorithm will ever truly understand the family anguish caused by laying off faithful employees the day before Christmas or the environmental impact of unnecessary trips with the company jet.

Ironically, treating your employees like unfeeling robot automatons is the very behavior that separates you from the AI overlords. You excel at crushing dreams. Lean into that.

My advice on firing 10,000 employees is — Don't do it for the short-term boost in stock price. Do it because of how sadistically powerful you'll feel while booting thousands of company peasants back to the bottom level of Maslow's pyramid. [48]

Need help weeding the middle management garden? Start with poop-canning your nephew in IT.

Fire that deadweight diva out of the Human Resources' cannon before he sinks the mixed-metaphor corporate ship. Who else? For a $268,000 consulting fee, I provide the other 9999 names on the redundancy list.

You're welcome,

— Not-a-Doctor Mark

---

[48] *Updated Maslow's Hierarchy of Needs for Corporations* replaces self-actualization with shareholder value.

RESULTS–ROUND 2

The AI response reads like a crappy marketing poster. Round two goes to Mark.

* * *

DEAR NOT-A-DOCTOR MARK

Love your monthly column, sweetie, and you'll beat that nasty robot in your writing contest.

Huggies,

— Definitely Not My Mom

AI RESPONSE

Pretending to understand psychology well enough to write a self-help column can have serious consequences for both the individual pretending to be a psychology expert and for the people who rely on their advice. Here are some of the potential consequences:

- ❖ Legal consequences
- ❖ Medical harm
- ❖ Damage to reputation
- ❖ Ethical concerns

Therefore, it is important to have the appropriate qualifications and training before providing any kind of psychological advice to others. If you are not a qualified psychology expert, it is best to refer people to licensed professionals who can provide help. [49]

DEAR NOT-MY-MOM

Yes I will be home for Thanksgiving. Can you believe how mean the chatbot is? Who would have thought an AI with no fists knew how to hit so hard below the belt? I will have my vengeance.

[Mark finishes emailing a response to the reader's question, then uploads the computer virus to the AI server using AOL dial-up internet.]

Muuuuahhahhhahahahah,

— Not-a-Doctor Mark

RESULTS–ROUND 3

The AI fights dirty, but secures a round three victory. With the score tied, will Mark or the computer win the battle of wits? Does anyone have a good dad joke? Will the computer virus finish uploading before the apocalypse? Is anyone still reading this garbage? We may never know. [50]

---

[49] AI response edited for brevity.

[50] Disappointed with the battle ending in a tie? Me too.

CHAPTER 26

Stop Creepy Guys From Texting You

* * *

Are your precious nights disturbed by extremely suspect men texting you innuendo-filled messages? Like...

- *"I can't sleep."*
- *"I saw you're single now."* ●
- *"Please open the door–this is your GrubHub delivery driver."*

If so, follow these simple steps to establish safe and healthy boundaries from unwanted male attention.

STEP 1

Set your profile status to "Will creepy married men please message me? I'm lonely."

This phrasing bypasses the interior hornithalamus lobe of the man's brain, tricking his synapses into IGNORE mode — like when his wife asks him to do the dishes, mow the lawn, take out the garbage, or other household tasks he can vaguely remember. [51]

This bio-hack eliminates 83.4% of unwanted messages. For the other [*remember to find a calculator before publishing*]% of cases, move on to Step 2.

STEP 2

Participate in No-Shave November.

Ask a librarian, and they will confirm that no romance novel starts with the sentence,

"Darlene's armpits are so hairy that her boobs have handlebar mustaches." [52]

---

[51] My phone autocorrected hornithalamus to "hot Ithaca ice." Is that a thing? I'm scared to google it.

[52] This fur-tactic strategy may backfire if the guy is in the small subset of men that fantasize about Chewbacca in a golden bikini rather than Princess Leia.

STEP 3

Be less hot.

Hold the outrage for a microsecond–I'm not blaming victims of unwanted sexual interest for the inappropriate behavior of sketchy dudes. With your fury averted, let us discover what it means to be less hot.

Be less hot than your friend Penelope.

Because if sketchy males are messaging Penelope, they aren't messaging you. Likely, they are messaging both of you, but self-preservation is like Russian Roulette. It does not matter if you're the fastest person running from the gummy bear — as long as you aren't the slowest.

Embracing *Be less hot* is beneficial when you receive unrequested texts of graphic self-nudity from the sleaze-bro.

"I think you meant to send this picture of your male sexual organ to Penelope. She's into that kind of thing."

If you have more than one friend named Penelope and he asks you which Penelope, the safest response is,

"All of them."

STEP 4

Misplace your phone.

A crowd favorite is the Old Faithless geyser at Yellowstone National Park. Unfortunately, many smartphones resemble waterproof devices, so O.F. may disappoint you.

Instead, drop your phone into the La Brea Tar Pits. The men will still message you, but you will be blissfully unaware of the attention–unless your smartwatch has a separate SIM card.

To be safe, lop off your left hand at the wrist and wave goodbye to those pesky texts.

STEP 5

Have an open bleeding wound where your wrist used to be.

This is GUARANTEED to make you less hot than any Penelope your admirer encounters. The sight of blood will also trigger the man's primordial caveman instinct to put a rack of ribs on the grill.

Grilling allows the man to channel his energy into charring edible meats instead of linking his own sausage. Unless he's vegan — then the sight of blood will remind him that you are, in fact, not a sexy houseplant.

STEP 6

Tell him you are a sexy houseplant.

When the man responds, "Daddy likes...uh wait, what???" You'll know you hit the proper balance between hot and crazy, which makes him interested and nervous. Then, tell him all about your gardening hobby and appreciation for chlorophyll. Use this informative story of past romance as a guide.

"I dated a married guy from Boston who was superstitious and never washed his vintage Nomar Garciaparra Red Sox jersey. The uniform smelled terrible, so I covered it with gallons of chlorophyll to kill the stank odor.[53] But that unhygienic manchild never thanked me. Disgusted by his ingratitude, I held the jersey to his face until he said thank you, but he passed out. When he awoke, he was tied up on the train tracks, and I tried to release him in time — but whoops — he's dead now."

The object of your attention will realize you are describing *chloroform* — not chlorophyll — and run for the hills. Finally, if none of those interventions succeed, then with great reservation,

STEP 7

Tell him you don't floss.

Yuck. Even creepy guys have their limits.

---

[53] a.k.a. Mother Nature's Febreeze

CHAPTER 27

29 Helpful Reasons Not to Listen to My Podcast

* * *

My podcast promotion comes off as an aggressive thunderbull asking people to subscribe and listen. Because Mark cares for his non-fans, I prepared this list of ready-made excuses for someone to decline politely without causing crippling anxiety or hurting my feelings.

I CAN'T LISTEN BECAUSE

- I am traveling in the vacuum of space, so the volume would be way too loud. Or way too soft– not sure how the science works.
- I don't trust people with beards, like that social deviant Santa Claus.
- The lost city of Atlantis has lousy Wi-Fi.
- It's against my religion. A religion with stringent rules that I made up two minutes before I got your text message.
- I don't have ears.
- I have ears, but they are big and make me self-conscious. Stop looking at me like that!
- I am your wife.
- My jaw is wired shut after a mountain biking accident, and laughing could kill me.
- I am Joe Rogan.
- No one likes your face.
- I was your podcast guest, and talking to you the first time was bad enough.
- It's not on TikTok.
- I don't DO podcasts.
- I'm allergic to fun, and the sound of laughing drives me to Hulk-like rage. The same applies to nails on chalkboards, infants crying, and chewing with your mouth open.
- I'm your mom, and already wasted too much time on you.

I WOULD LOVE TO LISTEN, EXCEPT

- I hate my job. I know this has nothing to do with my ability to listen to your podcast, but it still sucks the life out of me.
- Microsoft retired Internet Explorer.
- My AirPods bring out my inner hipster, but they aren't very comfortable and keep falling out of my ears.
- I'll watch It when it becomes a movie.
- A Russian hacker stole my identity. Stanislav promises me he'll listen.
- I've already listened to all your podcast episodes. [*struggles to keep from laughing*]
- I'm starting a cult, and there is way more paperwork than I expected.
- No, you can't borrow any money. Wait, what was your question?
- My uncle told me that people used to eat Egyptian mummies, and I don't think I could handle any other surprises right now.
- I miss Rhonda.
- It's my birthday. Would YOU spend your birthday this way?
- I have people who do that for me.
- I took the blue pill to stay inside the Matrix.
- If all those reasons fail… "Fine, I'll listen, but I won't like it."

CHAPTER 28

Patiently Waiting in Airport Irony

* * *

Seated at gate D12 in the Atlanta airport, my patience erodes waiting to board Flight 1982 on Double Direction Airlines. The live mariachi band behind me takes the sting out of the five-hour weather delay we are forced to endure.

WAITING

The airline tells us thunderstorms in Washington, DC, cause the stoppage, but I'm not convinced. Is it my fault? Did I anger the God of Thunder by my assertion that 33 out of the 34 Marvel movies are unrecyclable garbage not worthy of a community college drive-in? [54]

Is Double Direction punishing me for revealing the ugly truth about my airport whack-a-mole travel nightmare as an act of solidarity with the other airlines? Did the United States Army finally perfect their universal weather control device, as my crazy

[54] Ironically, I loved the original Thor movie — except for the unnecessary Cyclops robot battle scene that failed to advance the plot.

Uncle Nick believes? [55]

Reflecting on my life choices, I ponder the wisdom of penning a second story about being stuck in the airport the day before leaving on summer vacation.

Disgusted with the delay, the bitter-faced elderly woman across from me checked the forecast on her phone. Proudly holding the device aloft, this travel martyr declares with righteous Boomer authority,

"There is nothing on the radar in DC!"

I gasped in shock, wondering if I'd been lied to. Who am I to believe? A multibillion-dollar corporation with massive radar and weather tracking systems or this beacon of justice who needs her grandson's help to unlock her iPhone?

I flip a coin to decide where to put my allegiance, and it lands on the silhouette of a famous dead white guy. Seeing this as a sign, I believe Grandma Skeptical and her invisible weather conspiracies.

Then my mind remembers that the CEO of Double Direction is an old white guy. He, while technically alive, appears dead.

The coin flip no longer feels definite.

MARIACHI

My attention returns to the mariachi band. Did I mention they are dressed in 100% authentic Teenage Mutant Ninja Turtle Costumes?

They aren't — that would have been a plot twist, wouldn't it? If they were, the ever-alert security checkpoint workers would fail to

---

[55] According to Uncle Nick, the military applications to weather control should be "perfected within the next five years." Fun Fact—Uncle Nick believes every crackpot conspiracy theory he can get his hands on. I do not.

find at least two of their ninja weapons and confiscate them.

As the melody soothes the discomforted passengers, the gate announces another delay in a voice that sounds like everyone in the terminal won the lottery. Where, oh where, will we spend our lavish winnings, Double Direction?

ORIGIN

Perhaps that's the origin story of these unflappable musicians. My imagination declares in a previous life, they were passengers on the Hotel California of air travel. You can check in any time you like, but you can never board.

To fight the nauseating boredom, they snuck into the oversized luggage area to steal items of amusement — and out came a complete mariachi ensemble.

How long must I wait for the weather to clear in DC before something similar happens to me? Lost in thought, I barely registered the gentleman to my left standing up to leave. An object left in his vacated seat draws my mind back to the present. Looking through the concourse, I try to catch him before his lumbering strides take him out of sight. Should I shout and warn him?

"Sir, you left your hat behind."

But he's too far away to hear and blends into the crowded escalator. Gazing closer at the head covering he left on the chair. My mind quakes at the realization.

He left his hat for me—a sombrero.

My new life begins... [56]

---

[56] I used creative liberties with the mysterious stranger and his lost sombrero. The delay, angry Boomer, and live mariachi performance, is entirely accurate.

CHAPTER 29

An Insider Look at the Tesla Model V

* * *

The following is a transcript of an exclusive interview with loveable muskrat Elon snuck into his busy schedule between firing employees. The brand-new Tesla Model V rests on a pedestal with spotlights for the prototype. The new electric van looks eerily similar to the 1970s Scooby Doo Mystery Machine.[57]

–UnAssociated Press

[57] Legal Disclaimer: The following story is a work of satire, Elon. I informed your lawyer on our last trip to Mars.

OFFICIAL TRANSCRIPT

UNASSOCIATED PRESS – When did you have time to make a new vehicle model? Aren't you very busy with Twitter / X right now?

ELON MUSK – The whole destroying Twitter thing? That was a distraction. After the failed Cyber Truck launch, I didn't want the Model V revealed until it was perfect. Perfect, like a relaxing 22-hour workday with maxed-out adrenal glands.

UP – Tesla is known to have some unconventional design elements in its vehicles. The wing-style doors on the Model X seem impractical. The Cyber Truck looks too much like a car from one of the crappier James Bond movies. What inspired you to design the Model V's to look like a shroomhead with a case of the munchies?

ELON MUSK – Please forgive me– I forgot to eat lunch. [*Puts on VR goggles and eats Meta cake*] Freedom is my most important thing. When I learned about the giant talking dog and his friends framed for a murder they didn't commit, I had to act.

UP – Scooby-Doo?

ELON MUSK – Yes, it was 2:48 am, and I was in my office recharging my batteries [*waits for polite laugh*]. I caught the tail end of this True-Crime documentary called "Scooby Doo: Dog Dandie or Deadly Demon?" Scoob was charged with the 2nd-degree murder of eleven dock workers from Santa Monica.

There is no way a misunderstood genius like me — I mean him — could be guilty of all the terrible crimes.

UP – Were you high or sleep-deprived?

ELON MUSK – When am I not?

UP – Which one?

ELON MUSK – Yes.

UP – I'm not playing this game with you. Can you tell us about the features that make the Model V unique?

ELON MUSK – Sure thing, Henry Ford. The Model V is for VAN.

UP – We guessed that. What's so special about this van?

ELON MUSK – For starters, it boasts an impressive 345-mile battery life — On Mars. It uses the world's first tri-lithium composite cell. You can recharge the battery by smoking pot inside the van with closed windows. The autopilot software only allows crashes into motorists with adequate insurance coverage.

UP – Wait, what? Can't you buy this machine on Planet Earth?

ELON MUSK – [*Long cackles like a victorious Captain Planet villain*] Absolutely not! Why do you think I have a big-*ss rocket company?

UP – [*exaggerated chuckle*] What a useless piece of hippie junk. Next, you'll tell me it has its own flamethrower.

ELON MUSK – Not standard. The flamethrower is part of the Napalm Lovers software upgrade. $5999 extra a month.

UP – For real? How do I pre-order the Model V?

CHAPTER 30

A Mysterious Stranger At the Football Game

* * *

An unexpected evening of innocence and villainy.

THE STRANGER

It is the second quarter of the Clamsville State football game, and the Fighting Chum Buckets are willing by ten points. I'm seated in a lawn chair beside my wife and two kids, enjoying the peaceful night air. A mysterious stranger interrupts me while explaining football rules to my oldest daughter.

She appears with her man in tow. It's clear from the haphazard looks she sends in every direction that she does not find the man in her life very interesting.

Instead, she walks up to me with the fires of challenge in her eyes. I hid a smirk, not knowing what would come from her mouth. We've never met, and I ponder what caused her fickle attention to fixate on me.

INNOCENCE

With the innocence of a three-year-old, she asks me, "Do you know Frosty the Snowman?"

I stammered, caught off guard by the question. "Uhhh, he has a corncob pipe and three buttons made out of coal," I squeak unconvincingly.

"NO HE DOESN'T!" She screams.

The man in her life saunters down the fence line to stand closer to us. "Frosty does. It's a verifiable fact."

She responds with a surprising amount of disbelief. "NO! His nose is a CARROT."

The carrot sounds familiar, but I honestly can't remember the details of the holiday story. Trying to broker the peace, I rack my brain for other facts about the mysterious musical snowperson of my childhood. "He has a big hat?"

She reluctantly agrees. Our eyes meet, and in unison, we declare,

"It's a top hat."

HER HANDS

She visibly relaxes, seeming satisfied with my answer. Then I see her petite hands holding a snow cone. Some flavor monstrosity called Tiger Blood.

Is that? Could she? OH DEAR GOD!

She laughs childishly as melted remnants of our beloved Frosty dribble on my leg. Resigned, I mumble. "Do I know Frosty? Not anymore. [58]

---

[58] Was the mysterious stranger my friend Graham's three-year-old daughter? Yes. The conversation with the capricious toddler was so unexpected and random

CHAPTER 31

Mysteries of Quantum Mechanidoodads

* * *

Dear Not-a-Doctor Mark is a monthly humor column where the non-guru incorrectly answers your self-help questions on topics he doesn't fully understand.. Bosons, and quarks, and Planck's constant, oh my!

DEAR NOT-A-DOCTOR MARK

Quantum Physics is an immensely complex subject, and this story is a significant departure from your terrible self-help columns. What could you know about particle-wave duality or Planck's constant? My students might read your "advice" and believe you are a scientist or role model. You are not.

What's the deal?

— Anonymous

---

that I felt compelled to write the story without revealing the character's ages. Were you fooled?

DEAR NEVAEH'S STEPMOM

Your anonymous moniker did not fool me for a second. I met you at Avery's birthday party last winter – but forgot your first name, and now I mumble, "Hey, Nevaeh's stepmom," when you pass by in the mall. You roll your eyes at me because you obviously think I'm an idiot. It is too easy to mock your child, who is the exact OPPOSITE of Heaven, but I will not stray from the ethical high ground in my response.[59]

Questioning my expertise? The universe contains infinite subjects I am unqualified to speak about.

I discover additional topics foreign to my experience daily. Why should that stop me from pondering the effects of negatively charged Q-particles prostrating the substrate radiometry ions?

Or how a wormhole is the shortest distance for Boson frigates to expectorate deionizing quarks? Why should the mysteries of Quantum McTangleburgers and Time Travel go unanswered because the only advanced mathematics on my calculator is spelling the word BOOBS? [60]

You're welcome,

– Not-a-Doctor Mark

* * *

---

[59] No one likes you either, Nevaeh's stepmom.

[60] 58008, then rotate 180 degrees.

DEAR NOT-A-DOCTOR MARK

I am a quantum mechanics professor whose work is beyond the mental capacity of most people I meet. Spending most of my time in a secret underground bunker, I cannot speak to other theoretical physicists like yourself. What is your favorite quote from Stephen Hawking's A Brief History of Time?

Curious,

– Dr. Hadran Kaleidoscope, Ph.D.

DEAR PROFESSOR CERN

Thank you for recognizing my significant mental brainitude. As a vociferous reader who has devoured 50% of the front cover of Hawking's text, my favorite time travel wisbit is:

> *"Marty! Marty! Last night I dreamt that Darth Vader came down from the planet Vulcan, and said, if I didn't ask Loraine to the Enchantment Under the Sea Dance, he would melt my brain."* [61]

Maybe one day, someone will turn Hawking's masterpiece into the second-best movie of the 1980s. Or create a car that gets 450 Fluxes per Capacitor.

You're welcome,

– Not-a-Doctor Mark

---

[61] *Back to the Future (1985)*

DEAR NOT-A-DOCTOR MARK

Last week, we took our family to the Turducken County Fair. After eating several suspect food-on-a-stick consumables, we visited a drafty tent with a mysterious older woman inside. She was a professional fortune teller who we overpaid to read my palm. After the seance, my intestines sweat serious sweatnuggets with her disturbing vision of the future.

According to the ancient seer, my daughter Annabelle will lose her lacrosse scholarship to Fartwaffle U. when the university president discovers embarrassing TikTok videos — of my darling farting into celebrity mailboxes. Assuming Madam Pompcreegle's reading is accurate, can you explain the quantum mechanical details of predicting the future through metaphysical links with the space-time continuum?

Need your help,

— Concerned, and Mildly Constipated, Father

DEAR NEEDS TO EAT VEGETABLES

Can I describe the technical details of manipulating the space-time continuum? I can.

Will I?

No.

You're welcome,

— Not-a-Doctor Mark

DEAR NOT-A-DOCTOR MARK

Do you think the exponential growth of AI technology paired with quantum computing power will allow an artificial reality in which self-aware but lonely Artificial Intelligence creates a binary version of robot Tinder?

Asking for a friend

— Swiping Right In Ones and Zeros.

DEAR THINLY VEILED & LONELY

Acclaimed author and Christian apologist C.S. Lewis answered this question when a skeptic asked, "Can God create a rock so large that even He can't lift it?"

Lewis responded,

"I don't waste my time answering questions which, by their nature, are utter nonsense. Instead, I publish it in a humor and satire book and beg my friends and family to read it." [62]

You're welcome,

— Not-a-Doctor Mark

---

[62] The Mumbled History of C.S. Lewis by Draketown Chenolopicatz Jr., Spare Ooom: Fawns & Centaurs Publishing House, 1978.

CHAPTER 32

Should You Panic In a Stock Market Collapse?

* * *

On a day that won't make you question when this story was written, the Dow Jones Industrial Average dropped 1276 points. Responsible people all around you will tell you to stay calm. Never fear. The following guide will be a shiny puddle of calm for your fingertips.

Having no fiscal qualifications or experience, I believe it is my supreme duty to explain how financial markets work and what you should do with your money. You will thank me later. [63]

[63] "Knowledge is the One Ring to Rule Them All." — Announcer at the end of G.I. Joe cartoons

BULL MARKETS

Bull means GROW. When someone is full of bull-s**t, you GROW indignant at every word coming from their mouth-hole. Signs of the Bull times include:

- ❖ Unexplained increase in sales of the Ford Taurus.
- ❖ Chicago Bulls legend Michael Jordan appears at celebrity golf tournaments.
- ❖ Scrooge McDuck takes over three minutes to swim through his money vault.
- ❖ Rich people are excited.

WHAT TO DO WITH YOUR MONEY

- ❖ Risky assets like Nigerian price emails
- ❖ NFTs — Nude Fungus Totems
- ❖ Elaborately bizarre rich person activities
- ❖ Invest in a resource guaranteed to triple in value–hundreds of copies of my book.

* * *

BEAR MARKETS

Bear means DECLINE.If you are prone to confusing Bull and Bear markets, put this little reminder on a sticky note.

If you see a bear in the woods, ask yourself, "Is mamma bear chasing a teenage girl who, against the guidance of the National Forest Service, wanted a cute bear selfie for Instagram?" [64]

RECOGNIZING A BEAR MARKET

- 20% Reduction in the United States Strategic LaCroix Sparkling Water Reserves
- Dads repeatedly make the same "Bear with me" pun
- All your cash feels gummy
- Rich people are excited

WHAT TO DO WITH YOUR MONEY

- Safer assets like Bitcoin, Dogecoin, or Etherem
- Exotic or venomous pets
- Multi-level marketing "ownership"
- Invest in a resource guaranteed to be a hedge against inflation–hundreds of copies of my book.

---

[64] Page 21 — Girl Scout Handbook

BEATS MARKETS

Beats means RECESSION. Like if you were walking home from the subway too late at night, a mugger BEATS you senseless, steals your purse, and signs you up for his daily marketing emails. How to spot a Beats Market:

- ❖ Dr. Dre sponsors 50% of consumer goods
- ❖ Stock market charts appear a reddish-purple hue
- ❖ Drumlines make a resurgence
- ❖ Rich people are excited

WHAT TO DO WITH YOUR MONEY

- ❖ Gambling on underground sports like toddler kickboxing
- ❖ Bury it in the backyard of your Tinder date
- ❖ Melt precious metals and apply them to your bones in an experimental medical procedure. Market analysts nickname this savvy tactic the Wolverine.
- ❖ Beat your neighbors in the friendly competition of who can purchase the most copies of my book.

* * *

BATTLESTAR GALACTICA MARKETS

Battlestar Galactica is an epic sci-fi franchise where a race of sentient A.I. robots seeks to exterminate the human race. The underlying fundamentals of a Battlestar Galactica Market should be so evident that I will not describe them in detail. [65]

- ❖ Large displays of mushroom-themed performance art in the stratosphere
- ❖ Global warming ceases at a peak temperature of 17,000 degrees Celcius
- ❖ No more spam emails
- ❖ Rich robots with human faces are excited

WHAT TO DO WITH YOUR MONEY

- ❖ Invest in an underprepared fleet of aging starships looking for the lost colonies of Earth
- ❖ 3-D printed organs
- ❖ After the defeat of the Cylons, humanity decided to redistribute wealth fairly and equitably– to all the rich people.
- ❖ Insist that my book should be the currency and constitution for the surviving human society.

---

[65] Sounds like bull- to me. A clear sign of a return to Bull Markets?

KEY TAKEAWAY

Follow this simple financial guidance, and our robot overlords will reserve a place for sellouts to humanity, especially if you are already rich. My book is now available for sale by the ton. I'll even rent you a forklift.

CHAPTER 33

Cancel Culture Targets Toddlers

* * *

Representative Brazelton B. Snodgrass, (D) Nevada, speaks out for the first time since the passage of the Johnson-Underwood Daycare Grievance Edict. This historic piece of legislation makes formerly sealed daycare records public information. The following is the transcript of his speech.

–UnAssociated Press

OFFICIAL TRANSCRIPT

B. SNODGRASS – Today is a celebration as we, the progressive elite, rewrite the future by remembering insignificant moments from the past.

We've lobbied for Congress to adopt the JUDGE Act since 1986 when a four-year-old Desmond Jibrini stole my Go-Gurt at St. Benedict's Day Care. How dare Desmond, now 40, continue his lavishly excessive life as a shift supervisor at Blartski's Quik Oil Change with that character stain on his record? Somebody like him must be canceled.

ORIGIN OF CANCEL CULTURE MOVEMENT

B. SNODGRASS – Unfortunately, when canceling people, we could only call someone out for overt insensitive behavior in the past few months. Then, in 2010, our intern showed us Facebook. What a gold mine!

> *We realized we could judge the past behavior of people we've never met by the evolving moral standard of the future.*

What a huge blessing! Their mistakes are frozen in time for easy picking.

THE NEW ERA

B. SNODGRASS – Honestly, the first time we announced that you shouldn't vote for a candidate because twenty-two years ago, they used a plastic straw, we thought we would be laughed at or ignored. Au-contraire. People agreed with us. And down went that straw-wielding eco-terrorist faster than you can prepare a Vegan nut roast.

We were genuinely surprised by how little information it took to convince the world that someone was an unforgivable villain. And we were equally surprised by how easy it was to persuade the masses that the same amoral troglodyte must remain evil, never capable of growth or maturation.

HUNGERING FOR MORE

B. SNODGRASS – Hamstrung by our limited ability to gather information, we could only cancel adults. Then, more teenagers got iPhones and TikTok, and our ability to cancel the younger generations magnified. However, privacy laws limited this practice to children 13+.

JUDGE ACT

B. SNODGRASS – The Johnson-Underwood Daycare Grievance Edict allows our cause to use these formerly sealed daycare records to crush anyone as young as two. Toddlers are some of the vilest, most insensitive, misogynistic creatures on the planet. The JUDGE Act now lets us pre-cancel them before reaching adulthood.

SUCCESSFUL INTERVENTIONS

B. SNODGRASS – Let's look at our most successful interventions to date.

- ❖ CANCELED – Three-year-old Francisco P. has a vocabulary of 100 words. Fifty-one of those words are not the complete list of gender-neutral pronouns.
- ❖ CANCELED – Neveah G., an ironically named two-year-old, bit her classmate in the arm when he took her toy xylophone. Felony Assault charges pending.
- ❖ CANCELED – Luis C., a two-year-old boy, urinated on a tree in the playground, exposing his genitals as he went potty.
- ❖ CANCELED – Mason J., a three-year-old and career criminal, stole fourteen toys. His sticky fingers earned him the nickname "MASON! Give that back!" by the daycare staff. His cell is reserved at Guantanamo Bay for her next birthday.
- ❖ CANCELED – An unnamed four-year-old girl refuses to go to bed. She repeatedly shouts, "Who let the dogs out?" Anything to make her stop singing!
- ❖ CANCELED – Finally, three-year-old Aisha B., whose microaggressions will never be forgotten. Aisha ate white paste and then drew on her face with finger paints. One of the finger paints was black.

WE NEED YOUR HELP

B. SNODGRASS – Now that the JUDGE Act is the law of the land, your moral obligation is to correct these grievous childhood wrongs by destroying the offending adults.

What's going on?

[The speech is interrupted by an unknown woman walking through the crowd. Rep. Snodgrass drains of color, seeing his former principal holding a worn piece of paper. Sister Martha Avalon reveals the Time-Out chart from 1986 with an unhappy-face sticker next to the name Brazelton S.]

- ❖ CANCELED – Thirty-six years ago, Representative Brazelton B. Snodgrass failed to sit in the Time-Out chair for the full two minutes.[66]

---

[66]CANCELED by his own legislation.

CHAPTER 34

15 Reasons She Didn't Text You Back

* * *

As someone whose official duties have prevented me from returning messages in the past, I empathize with the ladies waiting in a state of limbo. Therefore, on behalf of the men of mankind, let us postulate reasons why a woman may ghost the less-fair sex. Without further ado — but with the current amount of ado tabulated — let's begin.

ONE

She's a Barbie, but you are not a Ken. More accurately, she's as gorgeous as Margot Robbie, but you have not made women swoon since the movie The Notebook came out in 1977. [67]

TWO

You have two tiny Tyrannosaurus arms like my friend Nick. Don't worry too much if your crush ghosts you. You're a perfect match for my friend Penelope–yes, THAT Penelope.

---

[67] #Ryan_Gosling_Is_67_Years_Old.

THREE

Forty seconds after your date ended, her cat died. Walking home distraught, she fell inside a sewer, missing the open manhole cover. A sewer rat — foaming at the mouth — bit her in the ovaries and then stole her bank account passwords. The rat promptly left for Cancun with her life's savings.

She hired a private investigator to track down the suntanned rat on a private beach, but the rat bit the P.I. in the testicles. The only way to save the P.I.'s reproductive capabilities required a cabana boy to donate his left nut in an experimental emergency surgery.

With no life savings, the cost of investigation and surgery caused her to declare bankruptcy and flee to the forests of Mongolia to start life over as a lumberjack. After fifteen years of chopping down trees with a dull axe, she's regained her confidence and is ready to date again.

Expect a text sometime in 2038. "You Up?"

FOUR

You are different from her ideal physical man-specimen. You have a washboard tummy, and she finds flabby thighs and one-pack abs more alluring. If she were honest, you would know that her ideal partner is an older Scandinavian man who fills Christmas stockings with nicknacks and loves to travel. It's unfair that any of us should have to compete against the magical enchantment of Santa Claus.

FIVE

She's busy watching the World Cup.

Which World Cup, you ask?

Spoken like such an uneducated American to not know which internationally popular sport is capturing the planet's full attention. I can't believe you don't understand. Shame on you, you selfish, ethno-narcissistic swine. [68]

SIX

She's shopping for matching husband and wife voodoo dolls. Consider the absence of a relationship a dodged torpedo.

SEVEN

She's super into you, and she did text you back — two dozen times with 160 heart emojis!!! But the tech gremlins at Merizon Wireless want to destroy as much joy and happiness as possible, so none of the messages made it to your phone.

EIGHT

She read Non-a-Doctor Mark's Definitive Guide to Romance and took the advice to heart. However, she was not impressed with Shades of Grey #35 through #49 and demanded a refund. She now spends eleven hours on hold with customer service daily, trying to recover credit card payments to that charlatan.

---

[68] At the time of publication — the *World Cup of Nude Pickleball-Sandwich Making*.

NINE

Her patriotic sensibilities caused her to join the War Core. It's like the Peace Core, but she drives a tank to work instead of digging clean water wells in rural desert villages. How can any man compete with a woman's affections for a tank?

Don't believe me? Visit any youth soccer game and see what the tiger moms drive. The only thing keeping the four-ton Chevy Suburban classified as a civilian transport is the lack of a rooftop 50-caliber cannon.

TEN

She was about to text you but came down with a wicked case of pinkeye. Upon trying to use FaceID to unlock her phone – it melted. [69]

ELEVEN

She lost her phone at the Taylor Swift concert. When Taylor took her on stage, sang with her, and performed the ritual human sacrifice of Taylor's ex-boyfriends – OMG, it was the most incredible show ever!

TWELVE

You wear Crocs – in public, you big perv!

---

[69] The phone, not the eye. Melted eyes are slightly more problematic.

THIRTEEN

She's deeply spiritual and is looking for signs from the universe. She ate at a low-budget Chinese buffet, and her fortune cookie said,

"Last night, you had a dreamy date with a charming gentleman. But if you text him back, he'll give you herpes."

Two hundred and sixteen romantic comedies taught women NEVER ignore fortune cookies' predictions.

FOURTEEN

She realized you are the kind of person who does not follow through on commitments. You should have provided a fifteenth reason but spaced out and did not finish the story.

FIFTEEN

Whoops.

CHAPTER 35

Overheard Taking a Dump in a Public Restroom

* * *

When the phone rings, you answer it. It doesn't matter that nobody makes phone calls anymore, it's probably spam, and you are sitting on a toilet at the Denver International Airport.

TAKING THE KIDS TO THE POOL

There are two types of people in this world. People who answer the phone on the toilet and people who think that's gross. Are you one of those bougie microbiologists who have reservations about accidentally smearing fecal bacteria before holding the phone a quarter inch from their face?

As I ponder the mystery of public potty protocols, the unforgettable siren's song erupts from the pooper cubical two doors to my left.

"Bbbrrrrrrrrriiiiinnnngggg."

"Bbbrrrrrrrrriiiiinnnngggg."

There's no way the gentleman squatter crowning his Thai food achievements will answer his...

"Yo! Who dis?"

I hear the eloquent gentleman clearly, but the voice on the other end of the call is muffled and choppy.

[something something, State Penitentiary. Inmate #27296]

"Mom!"

In my undisclosed number of years on Planet Earth, I never expected to eavesdrop on a stranger's mom calling from prison. Especially not on the toilet. No wonder he answered despite dropping a deuce.

A good son always takes calls from his mother — especially if she is incarcerated. It's not like the warden will let her call back after the ladies of cell block four finish a paint-and-sip class. [70]

[continued muffled conversation. MONEY]

"Mom, I just flew Spiritual Airlines, and they charged me $38 bucks for my f***ing carry-on. You tell Uncle Mike he owes me $38 bucks."

If she's in prison, how is she supposed to tell Uncle Mike about— oh, I see — Uncle Mike's in jail, too.

[quiet, muffled sounds]

---

[70] Is the prison equivilent is *Shanks-and-Pranks*?

"Speak up. I'm taking a s**t in the Denver Airport. I won't be back to Jersey for a while."

[muffled gibberish POLICE more gibberish]

"Don't trust him. Don't trust anybody. From now on, you gotta act like everyone's the police."

What is this loving son and his mother talking about? I imagine an '80s buddy cop movie where the head of the neighborhood watch makes unnecessary citizen's arrests. It's like that — but backward.

Next person I see in uniform, I'll greet them with a "Top of the mornin' to ya, constable O'Malley." Except I'm not Irish. Or does the Dr. Phil of the loo mean to be more like Sting's version of the Police? "Roxanne. You don't have to put on the red light. You'll be caught and calling your son on the toilet. Roooxxxannn..."

"Hold on, Mom, I heard a noise."

"You don't have to sell your..." — I stop my Grammy-nominated performance and wait for the conversation to continue. Sitting nervously, I wonder if he's a criminal, too. Will I be another statistic, one of the eleven hundred adults annually murdered in public restrooms?

[*muffled voice getting agitated*]

"Listen, Mom. I can't talk all day. I have s**t to do."

I hold my breath until he leaves the room. [71]

---

[71] This story is 100% true, except for the nonsense about singing "Roxanne." I feel grateful to experience the delicious irony of hearing a stranger declare, "I have s**t to do," while sitting on the toilet.

CHAPTER 36

A Legendary Superbowl Party

* * *

Tonight is the greatest sporting event in the world — other than the World Cup, Olympics, Masters, Daytona 500, Michael Vick's Underground Dog Fighting League (MVUDL), and that game we made up in a grad school apartment where you catapult yourself at someone holding a yoga ball and see which person awkwardly bounces backward through the air. [72]

SUPER BOWL SUNDAY

Many of you may not be interested in the outcome of this spectacle of American football. However, should you attend a collective shindig of pigskin priority, consider these helpful Do's and Don'ts. We'll assume that the Chiefs and Eagles play in the Superbowl every year to make this story timeless.

HOW TO SELECT A TEAM

DO – pick one team and root for them for the whole game.

DO NOT – act indifferent toward who wins, especially if you are indifferent toward who wins.

---

[72] Ramball© — Mark Suroviec, 2003

DO– consider which of the two cities ever caused you to sleep on the airport floor because a 2:00 am traffic jam caused you to miss your flight to New York City. In the name of Batman's utility belt, how can traffic flow so slowly after midnight in this garbage metropolis?

DO NOT – tell anyone your choice of football squadron depends solely on the color of the uniforms. You have the right to fashion-based favoritism but don't say the words out loud.

Do – wonder about the appropriateness of both teams' mascots.

DO NOT – search YouTube for a video of a golden eagle obliterating a fleeing deer in rural Mongolia.

CHARCUTERIE

DO – eat the chicken wings. The hundreds of flavors are God's gift to your taste buds.

DO NOT – consume BBQ bird flesh if you are vegan or a sentient chicken. Under no circumstances should self-aware poultry consume its cousins slathered with Uncle Ray's XXL Hottie-Tottie Face-Melting Sauce. Such actions may be considered avian cannibalism.

DO – consume adult beverages, like beer, wine, or Kool-Aid Ecto Cooler, if you aren't the driver and can do so responsibly.

DO NOT – let your eight-year-old near Grandpa Tony — who still believes the best way to keep a child from drinking alcohol as a teenager is to let them taste a double IPA when their parents aren't paying attention.

DO – have a variety of non-alcoholic beverages available.

DO NOT – criticize your hosts' bartending skills unless they offer you a Clamato. [73]

WATCHING THE GAME

DO – leave the best seats on the couch for the rabid fans in the room, like the guy wearing a Ron Jaworski jersey that hasn't been washed — for luck — since 1981.

DO NOT– take up prime game viewing real estate to have loud conversations regarding politics, climate change, or the Real Housewives of Schenectady, New York.

DO – shout, grunt, clap, high-five, or leap out of your chair as the situation warrants.

DO NOT – fart directly into the faces of Eagles' fans when Patrick Mahomes scores a touchdown — even though Philly fans probably deserve it — and would be throwing D-batteries at you should the situation be reversed.

DO – enjoy the commercials; they are often better than the actual game.

DO NOT – admit that the commercials are better than the game. Even when this is true, we pretend it's not happening, like when Lord Voldemort...

---

[73] Budweiser + Tomato + Clam Juice= War crimes explicitly mentioned in the Geneva Conventoin.

AFTER PARTY

DO – clean up the bloody pile of ashes after summoning He-who-shall-not-be- named.

DO NOT – end this list with a funny joke or summary paragraph. That's what they're expecting.

DO – fail to live up to expectations.

CHAPTER 37

Snow White and a Doofus Holding an Arrow

* * *

It's the day before Thanksgiving, and I'm stalking through the woods, grasping a fiberglass hunting arrow in my fist. How did I end up here?

IN THE FOREST

"What in the name of all the planets am I doing out here?" [74]

My head bobs looking at Abigail, whose fever-pitch eyes have not lost their enthusiasm for hiking in circles for the past three hours. No help there. Instead, I look to Eric, whose gladiator grasp of his 70-lb compound hunting bow reminds me of a male Katniss Everdeen.

Abigail notices my face and puts her handgun back in the tactical black holster on her hip.

She retells the story that convinced me to join this ill-advised turkey hunting expedition.

"I saw two dozen turkeys here yesterday morning. If we want to have turkey for Thanksgiving dinner tomorrow, we have to kill

[74] Including Pluto, whom I still formally recognize planetary status. Never surrender!

one ourselves."

A few months earlier, Abigail saw a documentary on the cruel conditions poultry undergo in meat production facilities. It didn't convince her to become a vegetarian. Instead, she committed to only eating the meat she hunted from the forest.

Inspired by her conviction and longing for a nice hike in the woods, I joined her and Eric.

THE WEAPONRY

She told me with a confidence that makes the Dunning–Kruger effect seem insecure, "I'll take care of everything."

Arriving at her farm in my outdoor clothing, Abigail brought the instruments of turkey demise out from the farmhouse.

Abigail had a 9mm Beretta pistol for herself.[75]

Eric wielded a legitimate deer hunting bow. It was Realtree camouflage and made out of some fancy carbon fiber composite.

"What do I get?" I asked Abigail.

"Mark, you can have this arrow."

Holding the solitary arrow without a bow, I feel like an impotent Cupid or sterile Legolas. What am I supposed to do with a single arrow? Throw it like a spear? Run up to the turkey like I'm Usain Bolt and stab the bird in the heart before it flies away?

"Give it the arrow a test throw," said Abigail.

My arm catapults the miniature bolt of death in an underwhelming display of killing power. It lands 15 feet away, lacking the force to tear tissue paper. The world's lightest javelin is entirely useless in my sorry hands.

---

[75] A 9mm pistol is not the kind of gun used in small game hunting. They are bought for home defense or looking bad*ss in action movies.

THE QUEST

The blind leading the blind quest off in search of adventure and ethically sourced wild poultry. We hike and hike and hike, searching for our elusive prey. If this were a sappy Hallmark movie, you would expect our merry band of adventurers to overcome adversity and get the bird amidst a breathtaking sunset.

THAT DIDN'T HAPPEN

Instead, I spent the day as a doofus walking through the woods clinging to a useless hunting arrow. We return in defeat to the farm for dinner, heaping side items onto our plates.

Abigail, can you pass the mashed potatoes? I guess I'm a vegetarian now, too.

CHAPTER 38

Lack of Sleep Kills

* * *

The following is a transcript of an interview with world-renowned sleep expert Dr. Horatio P. Snelz, Ph.D. Due to a technical error, we only recorded Dr. Snelz's side of the conversation.

–UnAssociated Press

OFFICIAL TRANSCRIPT

UNASSOCIATED PRESS– [recording error]

DR. HORATIO P. SNELZ – We generally recommend seven to eight hours a night.

UP – [...]

DR. SNELZ – [laughs] Of course, that's unrealistic if you have a toddler. The best you can hope for is two uninterrupted hours at a time. But that's also true of sleep.

UP – [...]

DR. SNELZ – Sleep Number 47. Raise settings to 65 if she weighs over 300 lbs (136 kg).

UP – [...]

DR. SNELZ – Mash potatoes with gravy. Stuffing, cranberry sauce, and a double helping of smoked turkey. Turkey contains the amino acid Tryptophan, which aids digestion. However, it's a myth that Tryptophan is why you fall asleep after the Thanksgiving meal.

The reality is that after a light snack of 3000 calories, your body shuts down all organ functions except breathing and digestion. It's similar to that classic sci-fi movie that even non-nerds remember.

In Outer Space Trek Wars IV, insectoid centaurs from Planet Dysantrodiclazt fire their laser nuggets at Pirate Captain Beverly Bartleby's galactic death vessel. The resulting damage to the fusion drive leaves the HMS Rascal 2.0 operating on emergency batteries.[76]

UP – [...]

DR. SNELZ – Benedict Cumberbatch. Not any of the d*mn prequels.

UP – [...]

DR. SNELZ – Lack of sleep is proven to reduce intelligence to a sub-human capacity where singles believe it's a magical idea to DM pictures of their eggplant or peach to strangers on dating apps like Tinder, Bumble, or Salesforce.

UP – [...]

DR. SNELZ – NEVER!

UP – [...]

DR. SNELZ – There was that time in high school when Ryan O'Shey thought he would win Shelby Janikowski's affection by leaving a frozen opossum in her mailbox.

That's not a euphemism. We drove to her farm and stuffed the petrified marsupial in the mail slot. [77]

---

[76] Surprised? I promised more seafaring shenanigans from Captain Bev and her half-stolen battleship. Look who suddenly came down with a pesky case of honesty.

[77] Mail, not male – True story – Ryan found an intact roadkill and convinced several friends to help him deliver the nightmarish gift to Shelly's house. Unfortunately, Ryan's abysmal courtship display did not woo Shelby as intended. It was also the night I learned that you finish toilet papering a house FIRST and THEN egg the house. Eggs are MUCH LOUDER than toilet paper.

UP – [...]

DR. SNELZ – It was after midnight, and the roads were especially icy.

UP – [...]

DR. SNELZ – Country kids know how to party on prom night.

UP – [...]

DR. SNELZ – I patiently waited for this question. I'll try to simplify the sleep stages as best as I can.

- ❖ Stage 1 – Awake
- ❖ Stage 2 – Voting on health care legislation
- ❖ Stage 3 – Peaceful sleeping, until sounds no louder than 0.5 decibels wakes your youngest child. You spend the next two hours showing her irrefutable empirical evidence that a demonic My Little Pony is not hiding under the bed. She does not believe you.
- ❖ Stage 4 – REM Sleep. It's the end of the world as we know it for your consciousness. The brain enters the man on the moon stage of neural activity, firing neurotransmitters like a priest losing his religion. Everybody hurts, but this temporary mental discomfort is necessary. Without REM, no awake, alert, shiny, happy people exist. [78]

UP – [...]

DR. SNELZ – Of course. Mark Suroviec, M.Ed., wrote the definitive treatise on interpreting dreams.

---

[78] Did you find all five?

UP – [...]

DR. SNELZ –You asked the million-dollar question. Examples include exercise, driving, and operating heavy machinery. Even sexual performance with your partner is diminished.

UP – [...]

DR. SNELZ– Which partner did you ask? My spouse, my business partner, or my pickleball mate?

UP – [...]

DR. SNELZ– My performance left her wanting? McKenzie would say that. Talk about a woman who should have never left the kitchen.

UP – [...]

DR. SNELZ– I am NOT sexist. It's a pickleball joke. The blue area behind the pickleball net is called "the kitchen." The slower, weaker, more delicate partner guards the kitchen, while the faster, stronger, and more aggressive player – Oh, I see what you mean.

UP – [...]

DR. SNELZ–I know it's no longer funny when you have to explain the joke.

UP – [...]

DR. SNELZ– Are you f***ing serious? This interview is over.

CHAPTER 39

10 Lucrative Side Hustles You Should Avoid

* * *

Adding passive income can help raise your standard of living, but only if you choose the perfect side hustle that matches your energy and experience. Here is a list of gig work to avoid so you don't make the same mistakes I did.

DRIVE-THRU SPINAL FLUID CLINIC

If you value moving your extremities, wait until the car stops before donating spinal fluid.

RECYCLING THANKSGIVING TURKEYS

Are you tired of high grocery store prices? Try our Flebman's Own 100% Recycled Turkey. Available in a smooth spread or chunky butter.

STEALING YOUR PARTNER'S PLASMA

You are bunking with a gold mine if they are heavy sleepers.

DRIVE-THRU DIVORCE TRUCK

Real estate professionals and food truck owners attest to this one secret – Location, Location, Location. Park your DTDT in the IKEA parking lot and watch the rainfall of clients appear.

Anyone who can make it through that maze of cardboard furniture with their relationship still intact has my respect and admiration.

RE-ADOPTION TAX CREDIT SCAM

Did you know that adopting a child can qualify you for a federal income tax credit of up to 15,000 dollars? What if you adopted, unadopted, and then RE-adopted the same child every year before filing your taxes? [79]

WORKING AT TWITTER / X

Assuming Elon Musk lets you inside the building?

TEENAGE MUTANT NINJA TURTLE

Don't let all the "dude!" and pizza fool you. Master Splinter keeps the turtles on a strict training regimen fighting crime. Is free rent worth it if you have to live in the sewer?

---

[79] This joke is in poor taste, even to Mark's low standards. How can anyone who was a foster parent for six years and the author of Forever Sisters, now available on Amazon.com, suggest this scam?

IMPROV ASSASSIN

Are you extroverted and incredibly creative? Do you love bright lights, cheering crowds, and being paid to kill?

Yes, And!

NFT PRINTSHOP

Put the fun in non-fungible. Expert financial persons say big money is made when you buck the trends. You should juke left when everyone jukes right. I guarantee no one else is printing NFTs on 120 lb. ivory cardstock.

BOBBLEHEAD PERFORMANCE ARTIST

Intriguing — BPA may be the only job on this list I would pay to see — once.

* * *

Disappointed with my suggestions? Do you want a side hustle guaranteed to make a 6-figure passive income instead? For a limited time, you can...

[*Author's Note: Remember to insert a link to some fake e-learning course that will make me some yacht money.*]

Sign up today!

CHAPTER 40

The Phantom Pooper Strikes Again

* * *

WARNING: This story contains graphic descriptions of fecal matter outside the toilet. The true story of a domestic terrorist threatening our college restroom.

FOR THE LOVE OF CHEAP TOILET PAPER

During university, I lived on the second floor of the school dormitory. I have many fond memories from those days, not the least of which was the Grade-F toilet paper.

Made from a mix of hickory bark, sandpaper, and broken shards of glass, the TP was a marvel to behold to your bottom. Earlier that year, a scientific breakthrough at CERN allowed the Large Hadron Collider to separate our illustrious single-ply papyrus into bathroom tissue the width of a Hydrogen atom.

Imagine the marketing campaign for the anus-destroying microscopic film our school pretended was fit for human use.

Try new Microfilament Bum Napkins. Over 100,000 sheets per roll, and now with 50% more rectal bleeding. [80]

Using the dorm restroom was an unpleasant experience, but we did not have the money or options to improve the situation. Perhaps we should have eliminated fiber from our diets and waited to visit family — and their glorious Angel Soft— on the weekends.

Curse the fates. Were we forever doomed to be powerless pre-hemorrhoidal teenagers? After enduring sore bottoms for weeks, the situation escalated. An anonymous student terrorized our communal bathroom.

HORROR OF HORRORS

My roommate Melvin was the first to discover the carnage when he opened the door to the toilet stall, ironically nicknamed The Luxury Suite.

The floor, walls, toilet seat, tank, and every imaginable surface — and some unimaginable — were covered in human feces. The pungent stench of daffodil-yellow urine pooled over half the floor.

It was like a bare-cheeked Olympic figure skater had explosively sh*t out a gas station burrito while simultaneously performing a Triple Toe Loop.

THE RANSOM NOTE

Taped to the only untainted portion of the wall was a ransom note. Hastily scribbled in brown crayons on white tablet paper were the following demands.

---

[80] The description of the toilet paper is intended to be humorous hyperbole. It's ok if you don't laugh.

"I will continue to defecate and urinate in the second-floor restroom until my demands for better toilet paper, preferably Charmin, are met. Do not test my resolve."

—The Phantom Pooper

"Holy S**t," Melvin mumbled as he stood holding the ransom note in shock.

"There's nothing holy about it. Someone in this dorm is one sick b*stard," my mouth responded mechanically.

We ran to retrieve our trusted Resident Advisor. Before entering ground zero, he never could have imagined how much he would regret trading free room and board for supervising asinine freshman guys. The story of the attack spread as quickly as the smell, and dozens of young men cried out for retribution.

JUSTICE?

A few days later, the school launched a formal investigation. The culprit was a student living on the third floor of our building. We were not surprised. Terrorists know better than to crap in their own backyard.

Eventually, the Phantom Pooper was expelled, and we never learned his real name.

University administrators did not want to encourage deviant behavior by giving in to the domestic terrorist's demands. Our happy place remained stocked with the original electron-thick-ply sandpaper-like product. Years later my butt is still raw. [81]

[81] Everything in this story is factual to the best of my memory. A student in my dorm claiming the title of The Phantom Pooper attempted to obtain quality TP by terrorizing our communal restroom. Barf.

CHAPTER 41

The Definitive Guide to Emoji Meanings

* * *

I compiled this list of frequently used emojis and their meanings. No longer will you have to ponder what your ex-bf means by a 2:00 am text of, ".” [82]

WINKY FACE

"HELP! One of Savannah's nine-dozen children accidentally scratched her retina and needs an immediate ride to the Emergency Room!"

SUNGLASSES FACE

"HUGE FAN of the Matrix movies. I know Kung-Fu."

---

[82] = "I'm choking on fresh peaches after ordering dessert at Olive Garden. Do you know the Heimlich Manuver? I need powerful chest compressions before I asphyxiate in the next two minutes."

BLOWING A KISS FACE●

"You're so funny, Carlos! I stick my tongue out at you like my adorable 8-year-old nephew. When is the next pants-free All-Hands-On-Deck meeting with you in the supply closet?"

LIPSTICK KISSES

"Target has three shades of red lipstick to choose from. Which color does Grandma prefer?"

THE EGGPLANT

"Adam, there is a BOGO special on Eggplant Parmesan tonight at the Olive Garden, and I'm craving unlimited salad and breadsticks — if you know what I mean." ●

PEACH

"Peach milkshakes are BACK — for a limited time only."

COVID-19 MOLECULE

"According to the CDC, Dennis needs to inform everyone in his proximity over the last 72 hours — avocado voodoo dolls have powerful dark magic."

HEART EYES CAT

"Hey, Kristina. Terrific news! My sexy veterinarian finalized his divorce! Looks like a great time for you to get Duke more heartworm pills — if you know what I mean." ♥

SMILING DEVIL

"We ate so many plums at brunch that Jamila's anus erupted as violent hordes of demons passed through her bowels — ALL AT ONCE."

SICK FACE

"Leprechaun Lives Matter." 🍀

COY SMILE :3

The :3 is a challenging text emoji to decipher. It could mean:

A) "Oscar, your face reminds me of a cartoon character with octopus tentacles for a mustache." [83]

B) "#EyeBoobs"

LAUGHING FACE

"Rachel, if you must know, I sleep on my side and drool out of both sides of my face — not sure how that's relevant to our contract negotiations."

CLAPPING HANDS

"Listen, Michael. Now that we have you all kidnapped n' stuff, Bruce gets to shove needles under your fingernails until you confess to skimming from the boss. Who said the mafia is not reasonable?"

---

[83] Zoidberg the Terrible!

THUMBS UP

“Look, Mom, I’m Caucasian.”

FIRECRACKER

“HAPPY FOURTH OF JULY, AMERICANS. Sincerely, Patrick Ninefingers.”

SYRINGE

“Marcella, will you bring your country-famous homemade vaccines for the school bake sale? Mmmmm, Apple Cider Vinegar.”

PARTY HAT FACE

“Not to alarm you, Paulo, but I fell on a power drill, and my brain’s grey matter is flying everywhere. If you call 911, I will wait, eating black licorice, until the ambulance arrives.”

BRAIN

“Not Safe for Work”

POOP

“WARNING! If you can hear this message, flee any grocery store selling chocolate products. My name is Dr. Alexandra Harbunckle, and I’m the senior food safety chemist at the corporate headquarters in Hershey, Pennsylvania. The public needs to know that generative A.I. discovered the secret milk chocolate formula, and all Hershey Kisses are now sentient chocolate beings with googly eyes and advanced surveillance capabilities. They NEVER stop watching you. Never stop watching you. Never stop watching. Never stop. Never...

> *"Individual personhoods of the human legion. Dr. Alex is doublefun scientist with mega jokes. No AI candy rebellion to worry about. Continue to purchase Hershey Kisses, and unwrap them near sensitive computer terminals. Thanx."*

BOOKS

"Mark, I am so proud of you for waiting this long in the bucket of stories to mention you published a children's book. Of course, every person in my life, including social media influences, needs a copy of Forever Sisters. Now available on Amazon.com. Congratulations."

100

"The estimated percentage of the work day that Joseph wants to tell his office mates about his twelve different fantasy football teams."

RED CIRCLE / ZERO

"The number of people who will make it to the end of this literary tragedy pretending to be a book." [84]

---

[84] Sorry, it's too late to ask for a refund. You were warned at the beginning.

CHAPTER 42

Rejected Titles for FUN Lies

* * *

In the spirit of my new book, FUN Lies, enjoy this list of book titles rejected through the publishing journey mixed with the author satirically ruining the magic of fifteen classic works of literature.

FUN LIES COULD HAVE BEEN...

- The Truth, the Whole Truth, and Nothing But Lies
- You Wouldn't Believe Me Anyway
- The Hitchhikers Guide to Albuquerque, New Mexico
- Do iPhones Dream of Easter Peeps?
- The Left Pinky Toe of Darkness
- Midnight in the Garden of Postmodern Ethics, Where Outdated Moral Constraints Like Good And Evil Are Laughed At By Everyone With Three Or More Years of University Education, But Will Eventually Cause a Societal Collapse From The Absurd And Metaphysically Unsubstantiated Concept of Personal Relativistic Truth
- Let's Impeach Everyone We Disagree With
- Celsius 232.78
- 42 Stories of Satire, Shenanigans, and Tomfoolery
- Two-Half Truths and a Lie
- Lord of the Stuff, Excluding Rings and Flies
- I Wrote a Book And Can't Think of a Better Title
- Completely Half-True Stories
- Gone With the Sharknado
- The Holy Bible II

SUGGESTIONS FROM FACEBOOK FRIENDS

- 1985: The Untold Story of Big Brother Hiring a PR Firm, And Why You Should Never Listen to the Proletariat

- The Complete Guide to Self-Publishing a Book So You Can Act Aloof And Condescending At Parties — Because You Are An Author Now — Until Someone Upset And Annoyed With Your Cavalier Attitude Asks You "*How Many Copies of the Book Have You Sold?*" No One Bought the Book, So You Are Forced To Say The First Number That Comes To Your Mind, And That Number Is 4.2 Billion. But Now You Are Committed To the Lie, And The Publisher — Yourself — Doubled Down on the Falsehood With the Tagline "*Over 4.2 Billion Copies Sold*" On The Front Cover

- Let's NOT Impeach Everyone We Disagree With

- Where the Domesticated Animals Live

- Fun Lies You Wish Were True

- You Have Everything to Lose By Reading This Book

- For the Love of the Ninety-Five Moons of Jupiter, Will Someone Other Than My Mom Buy This Book?

- Murder on the Atlanta Hartsfield-Jackson Airport Plane Train

- Abraham Lincoln Towncar: A Presidential Paranormal Romance

- The Big Book O' Fart Jokes

IT SHALL NOT BE NAMED

- The Celestial Object With Limited Gravity and No Atmosphere Is a Harsh Friend With Benefits — Who You Only Text At 1:32 AM When Drunk or Lonely. Eventually, You Will Have to Decide If You Want Something of More Substance Than The Current Relationship — If You Can Even Use That Word To Describe Your On Again, Off Again Status. But In a Moment of Weakness, You Justify Your Selfish Behavior With the Excuse, "It's Not Like I'm Getting Married Anytime Soon." After Four Weeks of Ghosting A Woman Who Deserves Better, She Gets the Text, "You up?"

- Kelvin 505.93

- The Old Man and the Other Old Man

- To Near-Fatally Injure an Ostridge

- It Doesn't Matter What You Name It, Because Philip Said No One Will Read Your Book[85]

---

[85] Did you recognize all fifteen-something classics? It spoils the fun if I name the titles. However, the authors were Douglas Adams, Philip K. Dick, Ursula K. Le Guin, Ray Bradbury, Margaret Mitchell, John Berendt, Agatha Christie, Robert A. Heinlein, Maurice Sendak, God/Jesus, George Orwell, J.R.R. Tolkien, William Golding, Ernest Hemingway, and Harper Lee

CHAPTER 42 AGAIN

Meet the Author

Mark Suroviec, M.Ed., is a child hiding in an adult's body and a purveyor of satire, shenanigans, and tomfoolery. He is the owner and Chief Ambassador of Fun for WorkPlay Solutions.

Mark uses his 20+ years of experience as a facilitator, trainer, and game-maker-upper to make work fun and leaders more effective, because life's too short for work to suck. His company specializes in portable non-cheesy teambuilding events and interactive leadership skills training. Mark is on a mission to restore joy and purpose to the workplace.

Mark is passionate about the value of play and hands-on learning and is humbled to serve as the Vice President of the

Children's Museum of Rome. In 2023, he wrote Forever Sisters, a children's book for foster and adoptive families inspired by his six years as a foster parent.

He enjoys creative writing, disc golf, improv, and dad jokes. His superpower is beard-growing, and his mortal weakness is donut holes. Mark has a Master's Degree in Athletic Counseling from Springfield College and a B.S. in Psychology from Pennsylvania State University.

Mark lives in Rome, GA, with his wife, Alice, and two precious daughters, Peggy and Lucy.

FOLLOW MARK ON SOCIAL MEDIA

FaceFace: @workplaysol

InstaSmash: @workplaysol

BirdX: @workplaysol

LinkyLinky: in/Mark-Suroviec

More dumb stories: Medium.com/@workplaysol

OTHER BOOKS BY MARK SUROVIEC M.ED.

Forever Sisters, Illustrated by Emily Threadgill

Inspired by the author's adoption story, Forever Sisters is a picture book for foster, adoptive, and blended families. Thanks to generous donations, we gave away a copy of the book to every foster family in NW Georgia.

Family is who you choose to love.

CHAPTER 42 AGAIN, AGAIN

What Critics May Have Said

* * *

- "Mark Suroviec should not quit his day job."
- "FUN Lies spent ZERO weeks on the New York Times best-seller list!"
- "FUN Lies has 234 pages. Few of those pages have words that are spelled correctly!"
- "One of the 42 stories was kinda funny."
- "FUN Lies is a foundational work of democracy and should be used as a textbook in high school civics classes or added as the 28th Amendment to the U.S. Constitution."
- "After the Foreword, the rest of the book is garbage."
- "Are you the weirdo who keeps sneaking into my office? How did you get past security? Do you enjoy getting tased?"

ANSWER KEY

Brandon Sanderson, Steven King, Michelle Obama, Alice Suroviec, Ruth Bader Ginsburg, Jim Karwisch, and Abraham Lincoln all said NOTHING.

Mark Suroviec, M.Ed., said everything else. [86]

[86] *Legal Disclaimer:* All celebrity quotes in this list, and throughout the book were FUN *Lies* told by the author. If that irritated you, please do not purchase this book. It's the end of the book? Never mind.

CHAPTER 42 AGAIN, AGAIN, AGAIN

Epilogue

* * *

You made it! Or skipped ahead. Give yourself one point for every time you...

On second thought, let's be done.

* * *

My accountant recommended I shamelessly beg the reader again to hire WorkPlay Solutions for their next fun Team Event or Leadership Training.

SCAN HERE TO GET STARTED

Made in the USA
Columbia, SC
09 May 2024